Tom Sawyer ABROAD

Here is one of Samuel Clemens' most beloved characters—and indeed one of the most delightful boys in all of literature—in another exciting and hilarious adventure.

When Tom and his friends Huck and Jim find themselves in accidental, but sole possession of a balloon, they are overcome by wanderlust and start on a series of journeys over the Atlantic Ocean in a machine which none of them has ever flown before! Flying over the Sahara Desert, the three travelers manage to anchor on a pyramid where they settle their problem in an unexpected though typically riotous manner.

Boys and girls who have laughed over the adventures of Tom Sawyer will enjoy catching up with their hero's incredible but always entertaining pranks.

*The professor never stirred till the sun
was overhead*

SAMUEL CLEMENS

Tom Sawyer
ABROAD

ILLUSTRATIONS BY
GERALD McCANN

COMPANION LIBRARY

Grosset & Dunlap

PUBLISHERS
NEW YORK

Contents

Illustrations

Tom Sawyer ABROAD

1: *Tom Seeks New Adventures*

Do you reckon Tom Sawyer was satisfied after all them adventures? I mean the adventures we had down the river, and the time we set the darky Jim free and Tom got shot in the leg. No, he wasn't. It only just p'isoned him for more. That was all the effect it had. You see, when we three came back up the river in glory, as you may say, from that long travel, and the village received us with a torchlight procession and speeches, and everybody hurrah'd and shouted, it made us heroes, and that was what Tom Sawyer had always been hankering to be.

For a while he *was* satisfied. Everybody made

much of him, and he tilted up his nose and stepped around the town as though he owned it. Some called him Tom Sawyer the Traveler, and that just swelled him up fit to bust. You see he laid over me and Jim considerable, because we only went down the river on a raft and came back by the steamboat, but Tom went by the steamboat both ways. The boys envied me and Jim a good deal, but land! they just knuckled to the dirt before TOM.

Well, I don't know; maybe he might have been satisfied if it hadn't been for old Nat Parsons, which was postmaster, and powerful long and slim, and kind o' good-hearted and silly, and bald-headed, on account of his age, and about the talkiest old cretur I ever see. For as much as thirty years he'd been the only man in the village that had a reputation—I mean a reputation for being a traveler, and of course he was mortal proud of it, and it was reckoned that in the course of that thirty years he had told about that journey over a million times and enjoyed it every time. And now comes along a boy not quite fifteen, and sets everybody admiring and gawking over *his* travels, and it just give the poor old man the high strikes. It made him sick to listen to Tom, and to hear the people say "My land!" "Did you ever!" "My goodness sakes alive!" and all such things; but he couldn't pull away from it, any more than a fly that's got its hind leg fast in the molasses. And always when Tom come to a rest, the poor old cretur would chip in on *his* same old travels and work them for all they were worth; but they were pretty faded, and didn't go for much, and it was pitiful to see. And then Tom would take another innings, and then the old man again— and so on, and so on, for an hour and more, each trying to beat out the other.

You see, Parsons' travels happened like this: When he first got to be postmaster and was green in the business, there come a letter for somebody he didn't know, and there wasn't any such person in the village. Well, he didn't know what to do, nor how to act, and there the letter stayed and stayed, week in and week out, till the bare sight of it gave him a conniption. The postage wasn't paid on it, and that was another thing to worry about. There wasn't any way to collect that ten cents, and he reckoned the gov'ment would hold him responsible for it and maybe turn him out besides, when they

*He had told about that journey over
a million times*

found he hadn't collected it. Well, at last he couldn't stand it any longer. He couldn't sleep nights, he couldn't eat, he was thinned down to a shadder, yet he dasn't ask anybody's advice, for the very person he asked for advice might go back on him and let the gov'ment know about the letter. He had the letter buried under the floor, but that did no good; if he happened to see a person standing over the place it'd give him the cold shivers, and loaded him up with suspicions, and he would sit up that night till the town was still and dark, and then he would sneak there and get it out and bury it in another place. Of course, people got to avoiding him and shaking their heads and whispering, because, the way he was looking and acting, they judged he had killed somebody or done something terrible, they didn't know what, and if he had been a stranger they would've lynched him.

Well, as I was saying, it got so he couldn't stand it any longer; so he made up his mind to pull out for Washington, and just go to the President of the United States and make a clean breast of the whole thing, not keeping back an atom, and then fetch the letter out and lay it before the whole gov'ment, and say, "Now, there she is—do with me what you're a mind to; though as heaven is my judge I am an innocent man and not deserving of the full penalties of the law and leaving behind me a family that must starve and yet hadn't a thing to do with it, which is the whole truth and I can swear to it."

So he did it. He had a little wee bit of steamboating, and some stage-coaching, but all the rest of the way was horseback, and it took him three weeks to get to Washington. He saw lots of land and lots of villages and four cities. He was gone 'most eight weeks, and there never was such a proud man in the village as he when he got back. His travels made him the greatest man in all that region, and the most talked about; and people come from as much as thirty miles back in the country, and from over in the Illinois bottoms, too, just to look at him—and there they'd stand and gawk, and he'd gabble. You never see anything like it.

Well, there wasn't any way now to settle which was the greatest traveler; some said it was Nat, some said it was Tom. Everybody allowed that Nat had seen the most longitude, but they had to give in that whatever Tom was short in longitude he had made up in latitude and climate. It was about a stand-off; so both of them had to whoop up their dangerous adventures, and try to get ahead *that* way. That bullet-wound in Tom's leg was a tough thing for Nat Parsons to buck against, but he bucked the best he could; and at a disadvantage, too, for Tom didn't set still as he'd orter done, to be fair, but always got up and sauntered around and worked his limp while Nat was painting up the adventure that *he* had in Washington; for Tom never let go that limp when his leg got well, but practiced it nights at home, and kept it good as new right along.

Nat's adventure was like this; I don't know how true it is: maybe he got it out of a paper, or somewhere, but I will say this for him, that he *did* know how to tell it. He could make anybody's flesh crawl, and he'd turn pale and hold his breath when he told it, and sometimes women and girls got so faint they couldn't stick it out. Well, it was this way, as near as I can remember:

He come a-loping into Washington, and put up his horse and shoved out to the President's house with his letter, and they told him the President was up to the Capitol, and just going to start for Philadelphia—not a minute to lose if he wanted to catch him. Nat 'most dropped, it made him so sick. His horse was put up, and he didn't know what *to* do. But just then along comes a darky driving an old ramshackly hack, and he see his chance. He rushes out and shouts: "A half a dollar if you git me to the Capitol in half an hour, and a quarter extra if you do it in twenty minutes!"

"Done!" says the darky.

Nat he jumped in and slammed the door, and away they went a-ripping and a-tearing over the roughest road a body ever see, and the racket of it was something awful. Nat passed his arms through the loops and hung on for life and death, but pretty soon the hack hit a rock and flew up in the air, and the bottom fell out, and when it come down Nat's feet was on the ground, and he see he was in the most desperate danger if he couldn't keep up with the hack. He was horrible scared, but he laid into his work for all he was worth, and hung tight to the arm-loops and made his legs fairly fly. He yelled and shouted to the driver to stop, and so did the

crowds along the street, for they could see his
legs spinning along under the coach, and his
head and shoulders bobbing inside through the
windows, and he was in awful danger; but the
more they all shouted the more the darky
whopped and yelled and lashed the horses and
shouted, "Don't you fret, I's gwine to git you
dah in time, boss; I's gwine to do it, sho'!" for
you see he thought they were all hurrying him
up, and, of course, he couldn't hear anything for
the racket he was making. And so they went
ripping along, and everybody just petrified to
see it; and when they got to the Capitol at last it
was the quickest trip that ever was made, and
everybody said so.

The horses laid down, and Nat dropped, all
tuckered out, and he was all dust and rags and
barefooted; but he was in time and just in time,
and caught the President and give him the letter,
and everything was all right, and the President
give him a free pardon on the spot, and Nat give
the darky two extra quarters instead of one, because he could see that if he hadn't had the hack
he wouldn't 'a' got there in time, nor anywhere
near it.

It *was* a powerful good adventure, and Tom

Sawyer had to work his bullet-wound mighty lively to hold his own against it.

Well, by and by Tom's glory got to paling down gradu'ly on account of other things turning up for the people to talk about—first a horse-race, and on top of that a house afire, and on top of that the circus, and on top of that the eclipse; and that started a revival, same as it always does, and by that time there wasn't any more talk about Tom, so to speak, and you never see a person so sick and disgusted.

Pretty soon he got to worrying and fretting right along day in and day out, and when I asked him what *was* he in such a state about, he said it 'most broke his heart to think how time was slipping away, and him getting older and older, and no wars breaking out and no way of making a name for himself that he could see. Now that is the way boys is always thinking, but he was the first one I ever heard come out and say it.

So then he set to work to get up a plan to make him celebrated; and pretty soon he struck it, and offered to take me and Jim in. Tom Sawyer was always free and generous that way. There's a-plenty of boys that's mighty good and friendly when *you've* got a good thing, but when a good thing happens to come their way they don't say a word to you, and try to hog it all. That warn't ever Tom Sawyer's way, I can say that for him. There's plenty of boys that will come hankering and groveling around you when you've got an apple and beg the core off of you; but when they've got one, and you beg for the core and remind them how you give them a core one time, they say thank you 'most to death, but there ain't a-going to be no core. But I notice they always git come up with; all you got to do is to wait.

Well, we went out in the woods on the hill, and Tom told us what it was. It was a crusade.

"What's a crusade?" I says.

He looked scornful, the way he's always done when he was ashamed of a person, and says:

"Huck Finn, do you mean to tell me you don't know what a crusade is?"

"No," says I, "I don't. And I don't care to, nuther. I've lived till now and done without it, and had my health, too. But as soon as you tell me, I'll know, and that's soon enough. I don't see any use in finding out things and clogging up my head with them when I mayn't ever have any occasion to use 'em.   There was Lance Williams, he learned how to talk Choctaw here till one come and dug his grave for him.   Now, then, what's a crusade?   But I can tell you one thing before you begin; if it's a patent-right, there's no money in it.   Bill Thompson he—"

"Patent-right!" says he.   "I never see such an idiot.   Why, a crusade is a kind of war."

I thought he must be losing his mind.   But no, he was in real earnest, and went right on, perfectly ca'm.

"A crusade is a war to recover the Holy Land from the paynim."

"Which Holy Land?"

"Why *the* Holy Land—there ain't but one."

"What do *we* want of it?"

"Why, can't you understand?   It's in the hands of the paynim, and it's our duty to take it away from them."

"How did we come to let them git hold of it?"

"We didn't come to let them git hold of it. They always had it."

"Why, Tom, then it must belong to them, don't it?"

"Why, of course it does.   Who said it didn't?"

I studied over it, but couldn't seem to git at the right of it, no way. I says:

"It's too many for me, Tom Sawyer. If I had a farm and it was mine, and another person wanted it, would it be right for him to—"

"Oh, shucks! you don't know enough to come in when it rains, Huck Finn. It ain't a farm, it's entirely different. You see, it's like this. They own the land, just the mere land, and that's all they *do* own; but it was our folks, our Jews and Christians, that made it holy, and so they haven't any business to be there defiling it. It's a shame, and we ought not to stand it a minute. We ought to march against them and take it away from them."

"Why, it does seem to me it's the most mixed-up thing I ever see! Now, if I had a farm and another person—"

"Don't I tell you it hasn't got anything to do with farming? Farming is business, just common low-down business: that's all it is, it's all you can say for it; but this is higher, this is religious, and totally different."

"Religious to go and take the land away from people that owns it?"

"Certainly; it's always been considered so."

Jim he shook his head, and says:

"Mars Tom, I reckon dey's a mistake about it somers—dey mos' sholy is. I's religious myself, en I knows plenty religious people, but I hain't run across none dat acts like dat."

It made Tom hot, and he says:

"Well, it's enough to make a body sick, such mullet-headed ignorance! If either of you'd read anything about history, you'd know that Richard Cur de Loon, and the Pope, and Godfrey de Bulleyn, and lots more of the most noble-hearted and pious people in the world, hacked and hammered at the paynims for more than two hundred years trying to take their land away from them, and swum neck-deep in blood the whole time—and yet here's a couple of sap-headed country yahoos out in the backwoods of Missouri setting themselves up to know more about the rights and wrongs of it than they did! Talk about cheek!"

Well, of course, that put a more different light on it, and me and Jim felt pretty cheap and ignorant, and wished we hadn't been quite so chipper. I couldn't say nothing, and Jim he couldn't for a while; then he says:

"Well, den, I reckon it's all right; beca'se ef

dey didn't know, dey ain't no use for po' ignorant folks like us to be trying to know; en so, ef
it's our duty, we got to go en tackle it en do de
bes' we can. Same time, I feel as sorry for dem
paynims as Mars Tom. De hard part gwine to
be to kill folks dat a body hain't been 'quainted
wid and dat hain't done him no harm. Dat's it,
you see. Ef we wuz to go 'mongst 'em, jist we
three, en say we's hungry, en ast 'em for a bite to
eat, why, maybe dey's jist like yuther people.
Don't you reckon dey is? Why, *dey'd* give it, I
know dey would, en den—"

"Then what?"

"Well, Mars Tom, my idea is like dis. It ain't
no use, we *can't* kill dem po' strangers dat ain't
doin' us no harm, till we've had practice—I
knows it perfectly well, Mars Tom—'deed I
knows it perfectly well. But ef we takes a' ax or
two, jist you en me en Huck, en slips acrost de
river tonight arter de moon's gone down, en
kills dat sick fam'ly dat's over on the Sny, en
burns dey house down, en—"

"Oh, you make me tired!" says Tom. "I
don't want to argue any more with people like
you and Huck Finn, that's always wandering
from the subject, and ain't got any more sense

than to try to reason out a thing that's pure theology by the laws that protect real estate!"

Now that's just where Tom Sawyer warn't fair. Jim didn't mean no harm, and I didn't mean no harm. We knowed well enough that he was right and we was wrong, and all we was after was to get at the *how* of it, and that was all; and the only reason he couldn't explain it so we could understand it was because we was ignorant—yes, and pretty dull, too, I ain't denying that; but, land! that ain't no crime, I should think.

But he wouldn't hear no more about it—just said if we had tackled the thing in the proper spirit, he would 'a' raised a couple of thousand knights and put them in steel armor from head to heel, and made me a lieutenant and Jim a sutler, and took the command himself and brushed the whole paynim outfit into the sea like flies and come back across the world in a glory like sunset. But he said we didn't know enough to take the chance when we had it, and he wouldn't ever offer it again. And he didn't. When he once got set, you couldn't budge him.

But I didn't care much. I am peaceable, and don't get up rows with people that ain't doing nothing to me. I allowed if the paynim was satisfied I was, and we would let it stand at that.

Now Tom he got all that notion out of Walter Scott's book, which he was always reading. And it *was* a wild notion, because in my opinion he never could've raised the men, and if he did, as like as not he would've got licked. I took the book and read all about it, and as near as I could make it out, most of the folks that shook farming to go crusading had a mighty rocky time of it.

2: *The Balloon Ascension*

WELL, Tom got up one thing after another, but they all had tender spots about 'em somewheres, and he had to shove 'em aside. So at last he was about in despair. Then the St. Louis papers begun to talk a good deal about the balloon that was going to sail to Europe, and Tom sort of thought he wanted to go down and see what it looked like, but couldn't make up his mind. But the papers went on talking, and so he allowed that maybe if he didn't go he mightn't ever have another chance to see a balloon; and next, he found out that Nat Parsons was going down to see it, and that decided him, of course.

He wasn't going to have Nat Parsons coming
back bragging about seeing the balloon, and him
having to listen to it and keep quiet. So he
wanted me and Jim to go too, and we went.

It was a noble big balloon, and had wings and
fans and all sorts of things, and wasn't like any
balloon you see in pictures. It was away out toward the edge of town, in a vacant lot, corner of
Twelfth Street; and there was a big crowd
around it, making fun of it, and making fun of
the man—a lean pale feller with that soft kind
of moonlight in his eyes, you know—and they
kept saying it wouldn't go. It made him hot to
hear them, and he would turn on them and
shake his fist and say they was animals and
blind, but some day they would find they had
stood face to face with one of the men that lifts
up nations and makes civilizations, and was too
dull to know it; and right here on this spot their
own children and grandchildren would build a
monument to him that would outlast a thousand years, but his name would outlast the
monument. And then the crowd would burst
out in a laugh again, and yell at him, and ask
him what was his name before he was married,
and what he would take to not do it, and what

It was a noble big balloon

was his sister's cat's grandmother's name, and all the things that a crowd says when they've got hold of a feller that they see they can plague. Well, some things they said *was* funny—yes, and mighty witty too, I ain't denying that—but all the same it warn't fair nor brave, all them people pitching on one, and they so glib and sharp, and him without any gift of talk to answer back with. But, good land! what did he want to sass back for? You see, it couldn't do him no good, and it was just nuts for them. They *had* him, you know. But that was his way. I reckon he couldn't help it; he was made so, I judge. He was a good enough sort of cretur, and hadn't no harm in him, and was just a genius, as the papers said, which wasn't his fault. We can't all be sound: we've got to be the way we're made. As near as I can make out, geniuses think they know it all, and so they won't take people's advice, but always go their own way, which makes everybody forsake them and despise them, and that is perfectly natural. If they was humbler, and listened and tried to learn, it would be better for them.

The part the professor was in was like a boat, and was big and roomy, and had watertight lockers around the inside to keep all sorts of things in, and a body could sit on them, and make beds on them, too. We went aboard, and there was twenty people there, snooping around and examining, and old Nat Parsons was there, too. The professor kept fussing around getting ready, and the people went ashore, drifting out one at a time, and old Nat he was the last. Of course it wouldn't do to let him go out behind *us*. We mustn't budge till he was gone, so we could be last ourselves.

But he was gone now, so it was time for us to follow. I heard a big shout, and turned around—the city was dropping from under us like a shot! It made me sick all through, I was so scared. Jim turned gray and couldn't say a word, and Tom didn't say nothing, but looked excited. The city went on dropping down, and down, and down; but we didn't seem to be doing nothing but just hang in the air and stand still. The houses got smaller and smaller, and the city pulled itself together, closer and closer, and the men and wagons got to looking like ants and bugs crawling around, and the streets like threads and cracks; and then it all kind of melted together, and there wasn't any city any

We didn't seem to be doing nothing but just hang in the air and stand still

more: it was only a big scar on the earth, and it seemed to me a body could see up the river and down the river about a thousand miles, though of course it wasn't so much. By and by the earth was a ball—just a round ball, of a dull color, with shiny stripes wriggling and winding around over it, which was rivers. The Widder Douglas always told me the earth was round like a ball, but I never took any stock in a lot of them superstitions o' hers, and of course I paid no attention to that one, because I could see myself that the world was the shape of a plate, and flat. I used to go up on the hill, and take a look around and prove it for myself, because I reckon the best way to get a sure thing on a fact is to go and examine for yourself, and not take anybody's say-so. But I had to give in now that the widder was right. That is, she was right as to the rest of the world, but she warn't right about the part our village is in; that part is the shape of a plate, and flat, I take my oath!

The professor had been quiet all this time, as if he was asleep; but he broke loose now, and he was mighty bitter. He says something like this:

"Idiots! They said it wouldn't go; and they

wanted to examine it, and spy around and get the secret of it out of me. But I beat them. Nobody knows the secret but me. Nobody knows what makes it move but me; and it's a new power—a new power, and a thousand times the strongest in the earth! Steam's foolishness to it! They said I couldn't go to Europe. To Europe! Why, there's power aboard to last five years, and feed for three months. They are fools! What do they know about it? Yes, and they said my airship was flimsy. Why, she's good for fifty years! I can sail the skies all my life if I want to, and steer where I please, though they laughed at that, and said I couldn't. Couldn't steer! Come here, boy; we'll see. You press these buttons as I tell you."

He made Tom steer the ship all about and every which way, and learnt him the whole thing in nearly no time; and Tom said it was perfectly easy. He made him fetch the ship down 'most to the earth, and had him spin her along so close to the Illinois prairies that a body could talk to the farmers, and hear everything they said perfectly plain; and he flung out printed bills to them that told about the balloon, and said it was going to Europe. Tom got so he could steer straight for a tree till he got nearly to it, and then dart up and skin right along over the top of it. Yes, and he showed Tom how to land her; and he done it first-rate, too, and set her down in the prairies as soft as wool. But the minute we started to skip out the professor says, "No, you don't!" and shot her up in the air again. It was awful. I begun to beg, and so did Jim; but it only give his temper a rise, and he begun to rage around and look wild out of his eyes, and I was scared of him.

Well, then he got on to his troubles again, and mourned and grumbled about the way he was treated, and couldn't seem to git over it, and especially people's saying his ship was flimsy. He scoffed at that, and at their saying she warn't simple and would be always getting out of order. Get out of order! That graveled him; he said that she couldn't any more get out of order than the solar sister.

He got worse and worse, and I never see a person take on so. It give me the cold shivers to see him, and so it did Jim. By and by he got to yelling and screaming, and then he swore the world shouldn't ever have his secret at all now, it had treated him so mean. He said he would

sail his balloon around the globe just to show
what he could do, and then he would sink it in
the sea, and sink us all along with it, too. Well,
it was the awfulest fix to be in, and here was
night coming on!

He give us something to eat, and made us go
to the other end of the boat, and he laid down
on a locker, where he could boss all the works,
and put his old pepper-box revolver under his
head, and said if anybody come fooling around
there trying to land her, he would kill him.

We set scrunched up together, and thought
considerable, but didn't say much—only just a
word once in a while when a body had to say
something or bust, we was *so* scared and worried. The night dragged along slow and lonesome. We was pretty low down, and the moonshine made everything soft and pretty, and the
farmhouses looked snug and homeful, and we
could hear the farm sounds, and wished we
could be down there; but, laws! we just slipped
along over them like a ghost, and never left a
track.

Away in the night, when all the sounds was
late sounds, and the air had a late feel, and a late
smell, too—about a two-o'clock feel, as near as I

could make out—Tom said the professor was so quiet this time he must be asleep, and we'd better—

"Better what?" I says in a whisper, and feeling sick all over, because I knowed what he was thinking about.

"Better slip back there and tie him, and land the ship," he says.

I says: "No, sir! Don't you budge, Tom Sawyer."

And Jim—well, Jim was kind o' gasping, he was so scared. He says:

"Oh, Mars Tom, *don't!* Ef you teches him, we's gone—we's gone sho'! I ain't gwine anear him, not for nothin' in dis worl'. Mars Tom, he's plumb crazy."

Tom whispers and says: "That's *why* we've got to do something. If he wasn't crazy I wouldn't give shucks to be anywhere but here; you couldn't hire me to get out—now that I've got used to this balloon and over the scare of being cut loose from the solid ground—if he was in his right mind. But it's no good politics, sailing around like this with a person that's out of his head, and says he's going round the world and then drown us all. We've *got* to do something, I tell you, and do it before he wakes up, too, or we mayn't ever get another chance. Come!"

But it made us turn cold and creepy just to think of it, and we said we wouldn't budge. So Tom was for slipping back there by himself to see if he couldn't get at the steering-gear and land the ship. We begged and begged him not to, but it warn't no use; so he got down on his hands and knees, and begun to crawl an inch at a time, we a-holding our breath and watching. After he got to the middle of the boat he crept slower than ever, and it did seem like years to me. But at last we see him get to the professor's head, and sort of raise up soft and look a good spell in his face and listen. Then we see him begin to inch along again toward the professor's feet where the steering-buttons was. Well, he got there all safe, and was reaching slow and steady toward the buttons, but he knocked down something that made a noise, and we see him slump down flat an' soft in the bottom, and lay still. The professor stirred, and says, "What's that?" But everybody kept dead still and quiet, and he begun to mutter and mumble and nestle, like a person that's going to wake up, and I thought I was going to die, I was so worried and scared.

Then a cloud slid over the moon, and I 'most cried, I was so glad. She buried herself deeper and deeper into the cloud, and it got so dark we couldn't see Tom. Then it began to sprinkle rain, and we could hear the professor fussing at his ropes and things and abusing the weather. We was afraid every minute he would touch Tom, and then we would be goners, and no help; but Tom was already on his way back, and when we felt his hands on our knees my breath stopped sudden, and my heart fell down 'mongst my other works, because I couldn't tell in the dark but it might be the professor, which I thought it *was*.

Dear! I was so glad to have him back that I was just as near happy as a person could be that was up in the air that way with a deranged man. You can't land a balloon in the dark, and so I hoped it would keep on raining, for I didn't want Tom to go meddling any more and make us so awful uncomfortable. Well, I got my wish. It drizzled and drizzled along the rest of the night, which wasn't long, though it did seem so; and at daybreak it cleared, and the world looked mighty soft and gray and pretty, and the forests and fields so good to see again, and the horses and cattle standing sober and thinking. Next, the sun come a-blazing up gay and splendid, and then we began to feel rusty and stretchy, and first we knowed we was all asleep.

3: *Tom Explains*

WE went to sleep about four o'clock, and woke up about eight. The professor was setting back there at his end, looking glum. He pitched us some breakfast, but he told us not to come abaft the midship compass. That was about the middle of the boat. Well, when you are sharp-set, and you eat and satisfy yourself, everything looks pretty different from what it done before. It makes a body feel pretty near comfortable, even when he is up in a balloon with a genius. We got to talking together.

There was one thing that kept bothering me, and by and by I says:

"Tom, didn't we start east?"

"Yes."

"How fast have we been going?"

"Well, you heard what the professor said when he was raging round. Sometimes, he said, we was making fifty miles an hour, sometimes ninety, sometimes a hundred; said that with a gale to help he could make three hundred any time, and said if he wanted the gale, and wanted it blowing the right direction, he only had to go up higher or down lower to find it."

"Well, then, it's just as I reckoned. The professor lied."

"Why?"

"Because if we was going so fast we ought to be past Illinois, oughtn't we?"

"Certainly."

"Well, we ain't."

"What's the reason we ain't?"

"I know by the color. We're right over Illinois yet. And you can see for yourself that Indiana ain't in sight."

"I wonder what's the matter with you, Huck. You know by the *color?*"

"Yes, of course I do."

"What's the color got to do with it?"

"It's got everything to do with it.   Illinois is green, Indiana is pink.   You show me any pink down here, if you can.   No, sir; it's green."

"Indiana *pink?*   Why, what a lie!"

"It ain't no lie; I've seen it on the map, and it's pink."

You never see a person so aggravated and disgusted.   He says:

"Well, if I was such a numskull as you, Huck Finn, I would jump over.   Seen it on the map! Huck Finn, did you reckon the states was the same color out-of-doors as they are on the map?"

"Tom Sawyer, what's a map for?   Ain't it to learn you facts?"

"Of course."

"Well, then, how's it going to do that if it tells lies?   That's what I want to know."

"Shucks, you muggins!   It don't tell lies."

"It don't, don't it?"

"No, it don't."

"All right, then; if it don't, there ain't no two states the same color.   You git around *that*, if you can, Tom Sawyer."

He see I had him, and Jim see it too; and I tell

you, I felt pretty good, for Tom Sawyer was always a hard person to git ahead of. Jim slapped his leg and says:

"I tell *you!* dat's smart, dat's right down smart. Ain't no use, Mars Tom; he got you *dis* time, sho'!" He slapped his leg again, and says, "My *lan'*, but it was smart one!"

I never felt so good in my life; and yet *I* didn't know I was saying anything much till it was out. I was just mooning along, perfectly careless, and not expecting anything was going to happen, and never *thinking* of such a thing at all, when, all of a sudden, out it came. Why, it was just as much a surprise to me as it was to any of them. It was just the same way it is when a person is munching along on a hunk of corn-pone, and not thinking about anything, and all of a sudden bites into a di'mond. Now all that *he* knows first off is that it's some kind of gravel he's bit into; but he don't find out it's a di'mond till he gits it out and brushes off the sand and crumbs and one thing or another, and has a look at it, and then he's surprised and glad—yes, and proud too; though when you come to look the thing straight in the eye, he ain't entitled to as much credit as he would 'a' been if he'd been *hunting* di'monds. You can see the difference easy if you think it over. You see, an accident, that way, ain't fairly as big a thing as a thing that's done a-purpose. Anybody could find that di'mond in that corn-pone; but mind you, it's got to be somebody that's got *that kind of a corn-pone*. That's where that feller's credit comes in, you see; and that's where mine comes in. I don't claim no great things—I don't reckon I could 'a' done it again—but I done it that time; that's all I claim. And I hadn't no more idea I could do such a thing, and warn't any more thinking about it or trying to, than you be this minute. Why, I was just as ca'm, a body couldn't be any ca'mer, and yet, all of a sudden, out it come. I've often thought of that time, and I can remember just the way everything looked, same as if it was only last week. I can see it all: beautiful rolling country with woods and fields and lakes for hundreds and hundreds of miles all around, and towns and villages scattered everywheres under us, here and there and yonder; and the professor mooning over a chart on his little table, and Tom's cap flopping in the rigging where it was hung up to dry. And one thing in particular was a bird right alongside, not ten foot off, going our way and trying to keep up, but losing ground all the time; and a railroad train doing the same thing down there, sliding among the trees and farms, and pouring out a long cloud of black smoke and now and then a little puff of white; and when the white was gone so long you had almost forgot it, you would hear a little faint toot, and that was the whistle. And we left the bird and the train both behind, 'way behind, and done it easy, too.

But Tom he was huffy, and said me and Jim was a couple of ignorant blatherskites, and then he says:

"Suppose there's a brown calf and a big brown dog, and an artist is making a picture of them. What is the *main* thing that that artist has got to do? He has got to paint them so you can tell them apart the minute you look at them, hain't he? Of course. Well, then, do you want him to go and paint *both* of them brown? Certainly you don't. He paints one of them blue, and then you can't make no mistake.

It's just the same with the maps. That's why they make every state a different color; it ain't to deceive you, it's to keep you from deceiving yourself."

But I couldn't see no argument about that, and neither could Jim. Jim shook his head, and says:

"Why, Mars Tom, if you knowed what chuckleheads dem painters is, you'd wait a long time before you'd fetch one er *dem* in to back up a fac'. I's gwine to tell you, den you kin see for you'self. I see one of 'em a-paintin' away, one day, down in ole Hank Wilson's back lot, en I went down to see, en he was paintin' dat old brindle cow wid de near horn gone—you knows de one I means. En I ast him what he's paintin' her for, en he say when he git her painted, de picture's wuth a hundred dollars. Mars Tom, he could 'a' got de cow fer fifteen, en I *tole* him so. Well, sah, if you'll b'lieve me, he jes' shuck his head, dat painter did, en went on a-dobbin'. Bless you, Mars Tom, *dey* don't know nothin'."

Tom lost his temper. I notice a person 'most always does that's got laid out in an argument. He told us to shut up, and maybe we'd feel better. Then he see a town clock away off down yonder, and he took up the glass and looked at it, and then looked at his silver turnip, and then at the clock, and then at the turnip again, and says:

"That's funny! That clock's near about an hour fast."

So he put up his turnip. Then he see another clock, and took a look, and it was an hour fast too. That puzzled him.

"That's a mighty curious thing," he says. "I don't understand it."

Then he took the glass and hunted up another clock, and sure enough it was an hour fast too. Then his eyes began to spread and his breath to come out kinder gaspy like, and he says: "Ger-reat Scott, it's the *longitude!*"

I says, considerably scared:

"Well, what's been and gone and happened now?"

"Why, the thing that's happened is that this old bladder has slid over Illinois and Indiana and Ohio like nothing, and this is the east end of Pennsylvania or New York, or somewheres around there."

"Tom Sawyer, you don't mean it!"

"Yes, I do, and it's dead sure.   We've covered about fifteen degrees of longitude since we left St. Louis yesterday afternoon, and them clocks are *right*.   We've come close on to eight hundred miles."

I didn't believe it, but it made the cold streaks trickle down my back just the same.   In my experience I knowed it wouldn't take much short of two weeks to do it down the Mississippi on a raft.

Jim was working his mind and studying. Pretty soon he says:

"Mars Tom, did you say dem clocks uz right?"

"Yes, they're right."

"Ain't yo' watch right, too?"

"She's right for St. Louis, but she's an hour wrong for here."

"Mars Tom, is you tryin' to let on dat de time ain't de *same* everywheres?"

"No, it ain't the same everywheres, by a long shot."

Jim looked distressed, and says:

"It grieves me to hear you talk like dat, Mars

Tom; I's right down ashamed to hear you talk like dat, arter de way you's been raised. Yassir, it'd break yo' aunt Polly's heart to hear you talk like dat."

Tom was astonished. He looked Jim over wondering, and didn't say nothing, and Jim went on:

"Mars Tom, who put de people out yonder in St. Louis? De Lord done it. Who put de people here whar we is? De Lord done it. Ain' dey bofe his children? 'Cose dey is. *Well,* den! is he gwine to *scriminate* 'twixt 'em?"

"Scriminate! I never heard such ignorance. There ain't no discriminating about it. The Lord made the day, and he made the night; but he didn't invent the hours, and he didn't distribute them around. Man did that."

"Mars Tom, is dat so? Man done it?"

"Certainly."

"Who tole him he could?"

"Nobody. He never asked."

Jim studied a minute, and says:

"Well, dat do beat me. I wouldn't 'a' tuck no sich resk. But some people ain't scared o' nothin'. Dey bangs right ahead; *dey* don't care what happens. So den dey's allays an hour's diff'unce everywhah, Mars Tom?"

"An hour? No! It's four minutes difference for every degree of longitude, you know. Fifteen of 'em's an hour, thirty of 'em's two hours, and so on. When it's one o'clock Tuesday morning in England, it's eight o'clock the night before in New York."

Jim moved a little way along the locker, and you could see he was insulted. He kept shaking his head and muttering, and so I slid along to him and patted him on the leg, and petted him up, and got him over the worst of his feelings, and then he says:

"Mars Tom talkin' sich talk as dat! Choosday in one place en Monday in t'other, bofe in the same day! Huck, dis ain't no place to joke —up here whah we is. Two days in one day! How you gwine to get two days inter one day? Can't git two hours inter one hour, kin you? Can't git two gallons of whisky inter a one-gallon jug, kin you? No, sir, 'twould strain de jug. Yes, en even den you couldn't, *I* don't believe. Why, looky here, Huck, s'posen de Choosday was New Year's—now den! is you gwine to tell me it's dis year in one place en las' year in t'other, bofe in de identical same minute? It's de beatenest rubbage! I can't stan' it—I can't stan' to hear tell 'bout it." Then he begun to shiver and turn gray, and Tom says:

"*Now* what's the matter? What's the trouble?"

Jim could hardly speak, but he says:

"Mars Tom, you ain't jokin', en it's *so?*"

"No, I'm not, and it *is* so."

Jim shivered again and says:

"Den dat Monday could be de las' day, en dey wouldn't be no las' day in England, en de dead wouldn't be called. We mustn't go over dah, Mars Tom. Please git him to turn back; I wants to be whah—"

All of a sudden we see something, and all jumped up, and forgot everything and begun to gaze. Tom says:

"Ain't that the—" He catched his breath, then says: "It *is,* sure as you live! It's the ocean!"

That made me and Jim catch our breath, too. Then we all stood petrified but happy, for none of us had ever seen an ocean, or ever expected to. Tom kept muttering:

"Atlantic Ocean—Atlantic. Land, don't it

sound great! And that's *it*—and *we* are looking at it—we! Why, it's just too splendid to believe!"

Then we see a big bank of black smoke; and when we got nearer, it was a city—and a monster she was, too, with a thick fringe of ships around one edge; and we wondered if it was New York, and begun to jaw and dispute about it, and, first we knowed, it slid from under us and went flying behind, and here we was, out over the very ocean itself, and going like a cyclone. Then we woke up, I tell you!

We made a break aft and raised a wail, and begun to beg the professor to turn back and land us, but he jerked out his pistol and motioned us back, and we went, but nobody will ever know how bad we felt.

The land was gone, all but a little streak, like a snake, away off on the edge of the water, and down under us was just ocean, ocean, ocean—millions of miles of it, heaving and pitching and squirming, and white sprays blowing from the wave-tops, and only a few ships in sight, wallowing around and laying over, first on one side and then on t'other, and sticking their bows under and then their sterns; and before long there warn't no ships at all, and we had the sky and the whole ocean to ourselves, and the roomiest place I ever see and the lonesomest.

4: *Storm*

AND it got lonesomer and lonesomer. There was the big sky up there, empty and awful deep; and the ocean down there without a thing on it but just the waves. All around us was a ring, where the sky and the water come together; yes, a monstrous big ring it was, and we right in the dead center of it—plumb in the center. We was racing along like a prairie-fire, but it never made any difference, we couldn't seem to git past that center no way. I couldn't see that we ever gained an inch on that ring. It made a body feel creepy, it was so curious and unaccountable.

Well, everything was so awful still that we got to talking in a very low voice, and kept on getting creepier and lonesomer and less and less talky, till at last the talk ran dry altogether, and we just set there and "thunk," as Jim calls it, and never said a word the longest time.

The professor never stirred till the sun was overhead; then he stood up and put a kind of triangle to his eye, and Tom said it was a sextant and he was taking the sun to see whereabouts the balloon was. Then he ciphered a little and looked in a book, and then he begun to carry on again. He said lots of wild things, and, among others, he said he would keep up this hundred-mile gait till the middle of tomorrow afternoon, and then he'd land in London.

We said we would be humbly thankful.

He was turning away, but he whirled around when we said that, and give us a long look of his blackest kind—one of the maliciousest and suspiciousest looks I ever see. Then he says:

"You want to leave me. Don't try to deny it."

We didn't know what to say, so we held in and didn't say nothing at all.

He went aft and set down, but he couldn't

seem to git that thing out of his mind. Every now and then he would rip out something about it, and try to make us answer him, but we dasn't.

It got lonesomer and lonesomer right along, and it did seem to me I couldn't stand it. It was still worse when night begun to come on. By and by Tom pinched me and whispers:

"Look!"

I took a glance aft, and see the professor taking a whet out of a bottle. I didn't like the looks of that. By and by he took another drink, and pretty soon he begun to sing. It was dark now, and getting black and stormy. He went on singing, wilder and wilder, and the thunder begun to mutter, and the wind to wheeze and moan among the ropes, and altogether it was awful. It got so black we couldn't see him any more, and wished we couldn't hear him, but we could. Then he got still; but he warn't still ten minutes till we got suspicious, and wished he would start up his noise again, so we could tell where he was. By and by there was a flash of lightning, and we see him start to get up, but he staggered and fell down. We heard him scream out in the dark:

"They don't want to go to England. All right, I'll change the course. They want to leave me. I know they do. Well, they shall— and *now!*"

I 'most died when he said that. Then he was still again—still so long I couldn't bear it, and it did seem to me the lightning wouldn't *ever* come again. But at last there was a blessed flash, and there he was, on his hands and knees crawling, and not four feet from us. My, but his eyes was terrible! He made a lunge for Tom, and says, "Overboard *you* go!" but it was already pitch-dark again, and I couldn't see whether he got him or not, and Tom didn't make a sound.

There was another long, horrible wait; then there was a flash, and I see Tom's head sink down outside the boat and disappear. He was on the rope-ladder that dangled down in the air from the gunnel. The professor let off a shout and jumped for him, and straight off it was pitch-dark again, and Jim groaned out, "Po' Mars Tom, he's a goner!" and made a jump for the professor, but the professor warn't there.

Then we heard a couple of terrible screams, and then another not so loud, and then another

He made a lunge for Tom, and says, "Overboard you go!"

that was 'way below, and you could only *just*
hear it; and I heard Jim say, "Po' Mars Tom!"

Then it was awful still, and I reckon a person
could 'a' counted four thousand before the next
flash come. When it come I see Jim on his
knees, with his arms on the locker and his face
buried in them, and he was crying. Before I
could look over the edge it was all dark again,
and I was glad, because I didn't want to see.
But when the next flash come, I was watching,
and down there I see somebody a-swinging in
the wind on the ladder, and it was Tom!

"Come up!" I shouts; "come up, Tom!"

His voice was so weak, and the wind roared
so, I couldn't make out what he said, but I
thought he asked was the professor up there. I
shouts:

"No, he's down in the ocean! Come up! Can
we help you?"

Of course, all this in the dark.

"Huck, who is you hollerin' at?"

"I'm hollerin' at Tom."

"Oh, Huck, how kin you act so, when you
know po' Mars Tom—" Then he let off an awful scream, and flung his head and his arms back
and let off another one, because there was a

white glare just then, and he had raised up his
face just in time to see Tom's, as white as snow,
rise above the gunnel and look him right in the
eye. He thought it was Tom's ghost, you see.

Tom clumb aboard, and when Jim found it
was him, and not his ghost, he hugged him, and
called him all sorts of loving names, and carried on like he was gone crazy, he was so glad.
Says I:

"What did you wait for, Tom? Why didn't
you come up at first?"

"I dasn't, Huck. I knowed somebody
plunged down past me, but I didn't know who it
was in the dark. It could 'a' been you, it could
'a' been Jim."

That was the way with Tom Sawyer—always
sound. He warn't coming up till he knowed
where the professor was.

The storm let go about this time with all its
might; and it was dreadful the way the thunder
boomed and tore, and the lightning glared out,
and the wind sung and screamed in the rigging,
and the rain come down. One second you
couldn't see your hand before you, and the next
you could count the threads in your coat-sleeve,
and see a whole wide desert of waves pitching

and tossing through a kind of veil of rain. A storm like that is the lovelist thing there is, but it ain't at its best when you are up in the sky and lost, and it's wet and lonesome, and there's just been a death in the family.

We set there huddled up in the bow, and talked low about the poor professor; and everybody was sorry for him, and sorry the world had made fun of him and treated him so harsh, when he was doing the best he could, and hadn't a friend nor nobody to encourage him and keep him from brooding his mind away and going deranged. There was plenty of clothes and blankets and everything at the other end, but we thought we'd ruther take the rain than go meddling back there.

5: *Land*

WE tried to make some plans, but we couldn't come to no agreement. Me and Jim was for turning around and going back home, but Tom allowed that by the time daylight come, so we could see our way, we would be so far toward England that we might as well go there, and come back in a ship, and have the glory of saying we done it.

About midnight the storm quit and the moon come out and lit up the ocean, and we begun to feel comfortable and drowsy; so we stretched out on the lockers and went to sleep, and never woke up again till sunup. The sea was sparkling like di'monds, and it was nice weather, and pretty soon our things was all dry again.

We went aft to find some breakfast, and the first thing we noticed was that there was a dim light burning in a compass back there under a hood. Then Tom was disturbed. He says:

"You know what that means, easy enough. It means that somebody has got to stay on watch and steer this thing the same as he would a ship, or she'll wander around and go wherever the wind wants her to."

"Well," I says, "what's she been doing since—er—since we had the accident?"

"Wandering," he says, kinder troubled—"wandering, without any doubt. She's in a wind now that's blowing her south of east. We don't know how long that's been going on, either."

So then he p'inted her east, and said he would hold her there till we rousted out the breakfast. The professor had laid in everything a body could want; he couldn't 'a' been better fixed. There wasn't no milk for the coffee, but there was water, and everything else you could want, and a charcoal stove and the fixings for it, and pipes and cigars and matches; and wine and

liquor, which warn't in our line; and books, and
maps, and charts, and an accordion; and furs,
and blankets, and no end of rubbish, like brass
beads and brass jewelry, which Tom said was a
sure sign that he had an idea of visiting among
savages. There was money, too. Yes, the professor was well enough fixed.

After breakfast Tom learned me and Jim
how to steer, and divided us all up into four-
hour watches, turn and turn about; and when
his watch was out I took his place, and he got
out the professor's papers and pens and wrote a
letter home to his aunt Polly, telling her everything that had happened to us, and dated it *"In
the Welkin, approaching England,"* and folded
it together and stuck it fast with a red wafer, and
directed it, and wrote above the direction, in
big writing, *"From Tom Sawyer, the Erronort,"*
and said it would stump old Nat Parsons, the
postmaster, when it come along in the mail. I
says:

"Tom Sawyer, this ain't no welkin; it's a balloon."

"Well, now, who *said* it was a welkin,
smarty?"

"You've wrote it on the letter, anyway."

"What of it? That don't mean that the balloon's the welkin."

"Oh, I thought it did. Well, then, what is a welkin?"

I see in a minute he was stuck. He raked and scraped around in his mind, but he couldn't find nothing, so he had to say:

"*I* don't know, and nobody don't know. It's just a word, and it's a mighty good word, too. There ain't many that lays over it. I don't believe there's *any* that does."

"Shucks!" I says. "But what does it *mean?* —that's the p'int."

"*I* don't know what it means, I tell you. It's a word that people uses for—for—well, its ornamental. They don't put ruffles on a shirt to keep a person warm, do they?"

"Course they don't."

"But they put them *on,* don't they?"

"Yes."

"All right, then; that letter I wrote is a shirt, and the welkin's the ruffle on it."

I judged that that would gravel Jim, and it did.

"Now, Mars Tom, it ain't no use to talk like dat; en, moreover, it's sinful. You knows a letter ain't no shirt, en dey ain't no ruffles on it, nuther. Dey ain't no place to put 'em on; you can't put 'em on, and dey wouldn't stay ef you did."

"Oh, *do* shut up, and wait till something's started that you know something about."

"Why, Mars Tom, sholy you can't mean to say I don't know about shirts, when, goodness knows, I's toted home de washin' ever sence—"

"I tell you, this hasn't got anything to *do* with shirts. I only—"

"Why, Mars Tom, you said yo'self dat a letter—"

"Do you want to drive me crazy? Keep still. I only used it as a metaphor."

That word kinder bricked us up for a minute. Then Jim says—rather timid, because he see Tom was getting pretty tetchy:

"Mars Tom, what is a metaphor?"

"A metaphor's a—well, it's a—a—a metaphor's an illustration." He see *that* didn't git home, so he tried again. "When I say birds of a feather flocks together, it's a metaphorical way of saying—"

"But dey *don't,* Mars Tom. No, sir, 'deed dey don't. Dey ain't no feathers dat's more alike den a bluebird en a jaybird, but ef you waits till you catches *dem* birds together, you'll—"

"Oh, give us a rest! you can't get the simplest little thing through your thick skull. Now don't bother me any more."

Jim was satisfied to stop. He was dreadful pleased with himself for catching Tom out. The minute Tom begun to talk about birds I judged he was a goner, because Jim knowed more about birds than both of us put together. You see, he had killed hundreds and hundreds of them, and that's the way to find out about birds. That's the way people does that writes books about birds, and loves them so that they'll go hungry and tired and take any amount of trouble to find a new bird and kill it. Their name is ornithologers, and I could have been an ornithologer myself, because I always loved birds and creatures; and I started out to learn how to be one, and I see a bird setting on a limb of a high tree, singing with its head tilted back and its mouth open, and before I thought I fired, and his song stopped and he fell straight down from the limb, all limp like a rag, and I run and picked him up and he was dead, and his body was warm in my hand, and his head rolled about this way and that, like his neck was broke, and there was a little white skin over his eyes, and one little drop of blood on the side of his head; and, laws! I couldn't see nothing more for the tears; and I hain't never murdered no creature since that warn't doing me no harm, and I ain't going to.

But I was aggravated about that welkin. I wanted to know. I got the subject up again, and then Tom explained, the best he could. He said when a person made a big speech the newspapers said the shouts of the people made the welkin ring. He said they always said that, but none of them ever told what it was, so he allowed it just meant outdoors and up high. Well, that seemed sensible enough, so I was satisfied, and said so. That pleased Tom and put him in a good humor again, and he says:

"Well, it's all right, then; and we'll let bygones be bygones. I don't know for certain what a welkin is, but when we land in London we'll make it ring, anyway, and don't you forget it."

He said an erronort was a person who sailed

around in balloons; and said it was a mighty
sight finer to be Tom Sawyer the Erronort than
to be Tom Sawyer the Traveler, and we would
be heard of all round the world, if we pulled
through all right, and so he wouldn't give
shucks to be a traveler now.

Toward the middle of the afternoon we got
everything ready to land, and we felt pretty
good, too, and proud; and we kept watching
with the glasses, like Columbus discovering
America. But we couldn't see nothing but
ocean. The afternoon wasted out and the sun
shut down, and still there warn't no land anywheres. We wondered what was the matter,
but reckoned it would come out all right, so we
went on steering east, but went up on a higher
level so we wouldn't hit any steeples or moun-
tains in the dark.

It was my watch till midnight, and then it was
Jim's; but Tom stayed up, because he said ship-
captains done that when they was making the
land, and didn't stand no regular watch.

Well, when daylight come, Jim give a shout,
and we jumped up and looked over, and there
was the land sure enough—land all around, as
far as you could see, and perfectly level and

yaller. We didn't know how long we'd been
over it. There warn't no trees, nor hills, nor
rocks, nor towns, and Tom and Jim had took it
for the sea. They took it for the sea in a dead
ca'm; but we was so high up, anyway, that if it
had been the sea and rough, it would 'a' looked
smooth, all the same, in the night, that way.

We was all in a powerful excitement now,
and grabbed the glasses and hunted everywheres for London, but couldn't find hair nor
hide of it, nor any other settlement—nor any
sign of a lake or a river, either. Tom was clean
beat. He said it warn't his notion of England;
he thought England looked like America, and
always had that idea. So he said we better have
breakfast, and then drop down and inquire the
quickest way to London. We cut the breakfast
pretty short, we was so impatient. As we
slanted along down, the weather began to moderate, and pretty soon we shed our furs. But it
kept *on* moderating, and in a precious little
while it was 'most too moderate. We was close
down now, and just blistering!

We settled down to within thirty foot of the
land—that is, it was land if sand is land; for this
wasn't anything but pure sand. Tom and me

clumb down the ladder and took a run to stretch
our legs, and it felt amazing good—that is, the
stretching did, but the sand scorched our feet
like hot embers. Next, we see somebody coming, and started to meet him; but we heard Jim
shout, and looked around and he was fairly
dancing, and making signs, and yelling. We
couldn't make out what he said, but we was
scared anyway, and begun to heel it back to the
balloon. When we got close enough, we under-
stood the words, and they made me sick:

"Run! Run fo' yo' life! Hit's a lion; I kin
see him thoo de glass! Run, boys; do please heel
it de bes' you kin. He's bu'sted outen de menagerie, en dey ain't nobody to stop him!"

It made Tom fly, but it took the stiffening all
out of my legs. I could only just gasp along the
way you do in a dream when there's a ghost
gaining on you.

Tom got to the ladder and shinned up it a
piece and waited for me; and as soon as I got a
foothold on it he shouted to Jim to soar away.
But Jim had clean lost his head, and said he had
forgot how. So Tom shinned along up and told
me to follow; but the lion was arriving, fetching
a most ghastly roar with every lope, and my legs

shook so I dasn't try to take one of them out of
the rounds for fear the other one would give
way under me.

But Tom was aboard by this time, and he
started the balloon up a little, and stopped it
again as soon as the end of the ladder was ten or
twelve feet above ground.   And there was
the lion, a-ripping around under me, and roaring and springing up in the air at the ladder,
and only missing it about a quarter of an inch, it
seemed to me.   It was delicious to be out of his
reach, perfectly delicious, and made me feel
good and thankful all up one side; but I was
hanging there helpless and couldn't climb, and
that made me feel perfectly wretched and miserable all down the other.   It is most seldom that
a person feels so mixed like that; and it is not to
be recommended, either.

Tom asked me what he'd better do, but I
didn't know.   He asked me if I could hold on
whilst he sailed away to a safe place and left the
lion behind.   I said I could if he didn't go no
higher than he was now; but if he went higher I
would lose my head and fall, sure.   So he said,
"Take a good grip," and he started.

"Don't go so fast," I shouted.   "It makes my
head swim."

The lion was arriving, fetching a most ghastly
roar with every lope

He had started like a lightning express. He slowed down, and we glided over the sand slower, but still in a kind of sickening way; for it *is* uncomfortable to see things sliding and gliding under you like that, and not a sound.

But pretty soon there was plenty of sound, for the lion was catching up. His noise fetched others. You could see them coming on the lope from every direction, and pretty soon there was a couple of dozen of them under me, jumping up at the ladder and snarling and snapping at each other; and so we went skimming along over the sand, and these fellers doing what they could to help us to not forgit the occasion; and then some other beasts come, without an invite, and they started a regular riot down there.

We see this plan was a mistake. We couldn't ever git away from them at this gait, and I couldn't hold on forever. So Tom took a think, and struck another idea. That was, to kill a lion with the pepper-box revolver, and then sail away while the others stopped to fight over the carcass. So he stopped the balloon still, and done it, and then we sailed off while the fuss was going on, and come down a quarter of a mile off, and they helped me aboard; but by the time we was out of reach again, that gang was on hand once more. And when they see we was really gone and they couldn't get us, they sat down on their hams and looked up at us so kind of disappointed that it was as much as a person could do not to see *their* side of the matter.

6: *It's a Caravan*

I WAS so weak that the only thing I wanted was a chance to lay down, so I made straight for my lockerbunk, and stretched myself out there. But a body couldn't get back his strength in no such oven as that, so Tom give the command to soar, and Jim started her aloft.

We had to go up a mile before we struck comfortable weather where it was breezy and pleasant and just right, and pretty soon I was all straight again. Tom had been setting quiet and thinking; but now he jumps up and says:

"I bet you a thousand to one *I* know where we are. We're in the Great Sahara, as sure as guns!"

He was so excited he couldn't hold still; but I wasn't. I says:

"Well, then, where's the Great Sahara? In England or in Scotland?"

" 'Tain't in either; it's in Africa."

Jim's eyes bugged out, and he begun to stare down with no end of interest, because that was where his originals come from; but I didn't more than half believe it. I couldn't, you know; it seemed too awful far away for us to have traveled.

But Tom was full of his discovery, as he called it, and said the lions and the sand meant the Great Desert, sure. He said he could 'a' found out, before we sighted land, that we was crowding the land somewheres, if he had thought of one thing; and when we asked him what, he said:

"These clocks. They're chronometers. You always read about them in sea-voyages. One of them is keeping Grinnage time, and the other is keeping St. Louis time, like my watch. When we left St. Louis it was four in the afternoon by my watch and this clock, and it was ten at night by this Grinnage clock. Well, at this time of the year the sun sets at about seven o'clock.

Now I noticed the time yesterday evening when the sun went down, and it was half-past five o'clock by the Grinnage clock, and half-past eleven A.M. by my watch and the other clock. You see, the sun rose and set by my watch in St. Louis, and the Grinnage clock was six hours fast; but we've come so far east that it comes within less than half an hour of setting by the Grinnage clock now, and I'm away out—more than four hours and a half out. You see, that meant that we was closing up on the longitude of Ireland, and would strike it before long if we was p'inted right—which we wasn't. No, sir, we've been a-wandering—wandering 'way down south of east, and it's my opinion we are in Africa. Look at this map. You see how the shoulder of Africa sticks out to the west. Think how fast we've traveled; if we had gone straight east we would be long past England by this time. You watch for noon, all of you, and we'll stand up, and when we can't cast a shadow we'll find that this Grinnage clock is coming mighty close to marking twelve. Yes, sir, I think we're in Africa; and it's just bully."

Jim was gazing down with the glass. He shook his head and says:

"Mars Tom, I reckon dey's a mistake somers. I hain't seen no darkies yit."

"That's nothing; they don't live in the desert. What is that, 'way off yonder? Gimme a glass."

He took a long look, and said it was like a black string stretched across the sand, but he couldn't guess what it was.

"Well," I says, "I reckon maybe you've got a chance now to find out whereabouts this balloon is, because as like as not that is one of these lines here, that's on the map, that you call meridians of longitude, and we can drop down and look at its number, and—"

"Oh, shucks, Huck Finn, I never see such a lunkhead as you. Did you s'pose there's meridians of longitude on the *earth?*"

"Tom Sawyer, they're set down on the map, and you know it perfectly well, and here they are, and you can see for yourself."

"Of course they're on the map, but that's nothing; there ain't any on the *ground*."

"Tom, do you know that to be so?"

"Certainly I do."

"Well, then, that map's a liar again. I never see such a liar as that map."

He fired up at that, and I was ready for him,

and Jim was warming his opinion, too, and next minute we'd 'a' broke loose on another argument, if Tom hadn't dropped the glass and begun to clap his hands like a maniac and sing out:

"Camels!—Camels!"

So I grabbed a glass and Jim, too, and took a look, but I was disappointed, and says:

"Camels your granny; they're spiders."

"Spiders in a desert, you shad? Spiders walking in a procession? You don't ever reflect, Huck Finn, and I reckon you really haven't got anything to reflect *with*. Don't you know we're as much as a mile up in the air, and that that string of crawlers is two or three miles away? Spiders, good land! Spiders as big as a cow? Perhaps you'd like to go down and milk one of 'em. But they're camels, just the same. It's a caravan, that's what it is, and it's a mile long."

"Well, then, let's go down and look at it. I don't believe in it, and ain't going to till I see it and know it."

"All right," he says, and give the command: "Lower away."

As we come slanting down into the hot weather, we could see that it was camels, sure

enough, plodding along, an everlasting string of
them, with bales strapped to them, and several
hundred men in long white robes, and a thing
like a shawl bound over their heads and hanging
down with tassels and fringes; and some of the
men had long guns and some hadn't, and some
was riding and some was walking. And the
weather—well, it was just roasting. And how
slow they did creep along! We swooped down
now, all of a sudden, and stopped about a hundred yards over their heads.

The men all set up a yell, and some of them
fell flat on their stomachs, some begun to fire
their guns at us, and the rest broke and scam-
pered every which way, and so did the camels.

We see that we was making trouble, so we
went up again about a mile, to the cool weather,
and watched them from there. It took them an
hour to get together and form the procession
again; then they started along, but we could see
by the glasses that they wasn't paying much attention to anything but us. We poked along,
looking down at them with the glasses, and by
and by we see a big sand mound, and something
like people the other side of it, and there was
something like a man laying on top of the

mound that raised his head up every now and
then, and seemed to be watching the caravan or
us, we didn't know which. As the caravan got
nearer, he sneaked down on the other side and
rushed to the other men and horses—for that is
what they was—and we see them mount in a
hurry; and next, here they come, like a house
afire, some with lances and some with long guns,
and all of them yelling the best they could.

They come a-tearing down onto the caravan,
and the next minute both sides crashed together
and was all mixed up, and there was such another popping of guns as you never heard, and
the air got so full of smoke you could only catch
glimpses of them struggling together. There
must 'a' been six hundred men in that battle,
and it was terrible to see. Then they broke up
into gangs and groups, fighting tooth and nail,
and scurrying and scampering around, and laying into each other like everything; and whenever the smoke cleared a little you could see
dead and wounded people and camels scattered
far and wide and all about, and camels racing off
in every direction.

At last the robbers see they couldn't win, so
their chief sounded a signal, and all that was left

of them broke away and went scampering across
the plain. The last man to go snatched up a
child and carried it off in front of him on his
horse, and a woman run screaming and begging
after him, and followed him away off across the
plain till she was separated a long ways from her
people; but it warn't no use, and she had to give
it up, and we see her sink down on the sand and
cover her face with her hands. Then Tom took
the hellum, and started for that yahoo, and we
come a-whizzing down and made a swoop, and
knocked him out of the saddle, child and all;
and he was jarred considerable, but the child
wasn't hurt, but laid there working its hands
and legs in the air like a tumblebug that's on its
back and can't turn over. The man went stag-
gering off to overtake his horse, and didn't know
what had hit him, for we was three or four hundred yards up in the air by this time.

We judged the woman would go and get the
child now; but she didn't. We could see her,
through the glass, still setting there, with her
head bowed down on her knees; so of course she
hadn't seen the performance, and thought her
child was clean gone with the man. She was
nearly a half a mile from her people, so we

thought we might go down to the child, which
was about a quarter of a mile beyond her, and
snake it to her before the caravan people could
git to us to do us any harm; and besides, we
reckoned they had enough business on their
hands for one while, anyway, with the wounded.
We thought we'd chance it, and we did.   We
swooped down and stopped, and Jim shinned
down the ladder and fetched up the kid, which
was a nice fat little thing, and in a noble good
humor, too, considering it was just out of a battle and been tumbled off of a horse; and then we
started for the mother, and stopped back of her
and tolerable near by, and Jim slipped down
and crept up easy, and when he was close back of
her the child goo-goo'd, the way a child does,
and she heard it, and whirled and fetched a
shriek of joy, and made a jump for the kid and
snatched it and hugged it, and dropped it and
hugged Jim, and then snatched off a gold chain
and hung it around Jim's neck, and hugged him
again, and jerked up the child again, a-sobbing
and glorifying all the time; and Jim he shoved
for the ladder and up it, and in a minute we was
back up in the sky and the woman was staring
up, with the back of her head between her

*Jim slipped down and crept up easy, and she
made a jump for the child*

shoulders and the child with its arms locked around her neck. And there she stood, as long as we was in sight a-sailing away in the sky.

7: *Tom Respects the Flea*

"NOON!" says Tom, and so it was. His shadder was just a blot around his feet. We looked, and the Grinnage clock was so close to twelve the difference didn't amount to nothing. So Tom said London was right north of us or right south of us, one or t'other, and he reckoned by the weather and the sand and the camels it was north; and a good many miles north, too; as many as from New York to the city of Mexico, he guessed.

Jim said he reckoned a balloon was a good deal the fastest thing in the world, unless it might be some kinds of birds—a wild pigeon, maybe, or a railroad.

But Tom said he had read about railroads in England going nearly a hundred miles an hour for a little ways, and there never was a bird in the world that could do that—except one, and that was a flea.

"A flea? Why, Mars Tom, in de fust place he ain't a bird, strickly speakin'—"

"He ain't a bird, eh?   Well, then, what is he?"

"I don't rightly know, Mars Tom, but I speck he's only jist a' animal.   No, I reckon dat won't do, nuther, he ain't big enough for a' animal. He mus' be a bug.   Yassir, dat's what he is, he's a bug."

"I bet he ain't, but let it go.   What's your second place?"

"Well, in de second place, birds is creturs dat goes a long ways, but a flea don't."

"He don't, don't he?   Come, now, what is a long distance if you know?"

"Why, it's miles, and lots of 'em—anybody knows dat."

"Can't a man walk miles?"

"Yassir, he kin."

"As many as a railroad?"

"Yassir, if you give him time."

"Can't a flea?"

"Well—I s'pose so—ef you gives him heaps of time."

"Now you begin to see, don't you, that *distance* ain't the thing to judge by, at all; it's the time it takes to go the distance *in* that *counts,* ain't it?"

"Well, hit do look sorter so, but I wouldn't 'a' b'lieved it, Mars Tom."

"It's a matter of *proportion*, that's what it is; and when you come to gauge a thing's speed by its size, where's your bird and your man and your railroad 'longside of a flea? The fastest man can't run more than about ten miles in an hour—not much over ten thousand times his own length. But all the books says any common ordinary third-class flea can jump a hundred and fifty times his own length; yes, and he can make five jumps a second too—seven hundred and fifty times his own length, in one little second—for he don't fool away any time stopping and starting—he does them both at the same time; you'll see, if you try to put your finger on him. Now that's a common, ordinary, third-class flea's gait; but you take an Eyetalian *first*-class, that's been the pet of the nobility all his life, and hasn't ever known what want or sickness or exposure was, and he can jump more than three hundred times his own length, and keep it up all day, five such jumps every second, which is fifteen hundred times his own length. Well, suppose a man could go fifteen hundred times his own length in a second—say, a mile and a half. It's ninety miles a minute; it's considerable more than five thousand miles an hour. Where's your man *now?*—yes, and your bird, and your railroad, and your balloon? Laws, they don't amount to shucks 'longside of a flea. A flea is just a comet b'iled down small."

Jim was a good deal astonished, and so was I. Jim said:

"Is dem figgers jist edjackly true, en no jokin' en no lies, Mars Tom?"

"Yes, they are; they're perfectly true."

"Well, den, honey, a body's got to respec' a flea. I ain't had no respec' for um befo', sca'sely, but dey ain't no gittin' roun' it, dey do deserve it, dat's certain."

"Well, I bet they do. They've got ever so much more sense, and brains, and brightness, in proportion to their size, than any other cretur in the world. A person can learn them 'most anything; and they learn it quicker than any other cretur, too. They've been learnt to haul little carriages in harness, and go this way and that way and t'other way according to their orders; yes, and to march and drill like soldiers, doing it as exact, according to orders, as soldiers does it. They've been learnt to do all sorts of hard and troublesome things. S'pose you could cultivate a flea up to the size of a man, and keep his natural smartness a-growing and a-growing right along up, bigger and bigger, and keener and keener, in the same proportion—where'd the human race be, do you reckon? That flea would be President of the United States, and you couldn't any more prevent it than you can prevent lightning."

"My lan', Mars Tom, I never knowed dey was so much *to* de beas'. No, sir, I never had no idea of it, and dat's de fac'."

"There's more to him, by a long sight, than there is to any other cretur, man or beast, in proportion to size. He's the interestingest of them all. People have so much to say about an ant's strength, and an elephant's, and a locomotive's. Shucks, they don't begin with a flea. He can lift two or three hundred times his own weight. And none of them can come anywhere near it. And, moreover, he has got notions of his own, and is very particular, and you can't fool him; his instinct, or his judgment, or whatever it is, is perfectly sound and clear, and don't ever make a mistake. People think all humans are alike to a flea. It ain't so. There's folks that he won't go near, hungry or not hungry, and I'm one of them. I've never had one of them on me in my life."

"Mars Tom!"

"It's so; I ain't joking."

"Well, sah, I hain't ever heard de likes o' dat befo'."

Jim couldn't believe it, and I couldn't; so we had to drop down to the sand and git a supply and see. Tom was right. They went for me and Jim by the thousand, but not a one of them lit on Tom. There warn't no explaining it, but there it was and there warn't no getting around it. He said it had always been just so, and he'd just as soon be where there was a million of them as not; they'd never touch him nor bother him.

We went up to the cold weather to freeze 'em out, and stayed a little spell, and then come back to the comfortable weather and went lazying along twenty or twenty-five miles an hour, the way we'd been doing for the last few hours. The reason was, that the longer we was in that solemn, peaceful desert, the more the hurry and fuss got kind of soothed down in us, and the more happier and contented and satisfied we got to feeling, and the more we got to liking the desert, and then loving it. So we had cramped the speed down, as I was saying, and was having a most noble good lazy time, sometimes watching through the glasses, sometimes stretched out on the lockers reading, sometimes taking a nap.

It didn't seem like we was the same lot that was in such a state to find land and git ashore, but it was. But we had got over that—clean over it. We was used to the balloon now and not afraid any more, and didn't want to be anywheres else. Why, it seemed just like home; it 'most seemed as if I had been born and raised in it, and Jim and Tom said the same. And always I had had hateful people around me, a-nagging at me, and pestering of me, and scolding, and finding fault, and fussing and bothering, and sticking to me, and keeping after me, and making me do this, and making me do that and

t'other, and always selecting out the things I
didn't want to do, and then giving me Sam Hill
because I shirked and done something else, and
just aggravating the life out of a body all the
time; but up here in the sky it was so still and
sunshiny and lovely, and plenty to eat, and
plenty of sleep, and strange things to see, and no
nagging and no pestering, and no good people,
and just holiday all the time. Land, I warn't in
no hurry to git out and buck at civilization
again. Now, one of the worst things about civilization is, that anybody that gits a letter with
trouble in it comes and tells you all about it and
makes you feel bad, and the newspapers fetches
you the troubles of everybody all over the
world, and keeps you downhearted and dismal
'most all the time, and it's such a heavy load for
a person. I hate them newspapers; and I hate
letters; and if I had my way I wouldn't allow
nobody to load his troubles onto other folks he
ain't acquainted with, on t'other side of
the world, that way. Well, up in a balloon
there ain't any of that, and it's the darlingest
place there is.

We had supper, and that night was one of the
prettiest nights I ever see. The moon made it

just like daylight, only a heap softer; and once
we see a lion standing all alone by himself, just
all alone on the earth, it seemed like, and his
shadder laid on the sand by him like a puddle of
ink. That's the kind of moonlight to have.

Mainly we laid on our backs and talked; we
didn't want to go to sleep. Tom said we was
right in the midst of the *Arabian Nights* now.
He said it was right along here that one of the
cutest things in that book happened; so we
looked down and watched while he told about
it, because there ain't anything that is so interesting to look at as a place that a book has talked
about. It was a tale about a camel-driver that
had lost his camel, and he come along in the
desert and met a man, and says:

"Have you run across a stray camel today?"

And the man says:

"Was he blind in his left eye?"

"Yes."

"Had he lost an upper front tooth?"

"Yes."

"Was his off hind leg lame?"

"Yes."

"Was he loaded with millet-seed on one side
and honey on the other?"

"Yes, but you needn't go into no more details —that's the one, and I'm in a hurry. Where did you see him?"

"I hain't seen him at all," the man says.

"Hain't seen him at all? How can you describe him so close, then?"

"Because when a person knows how to use his eyes, everything has got a meaning to it; but most people's eyes ain't any good to them. I knowed a camel had been along, because I seen his track. I knowed he was lame in his off hind leg because he had favored that foot and trod light on it, and his track showed it. I knowed he was blind on his left side because he only nibbled the grass on the right side of the trail. I knowed he had lost an upper front tooth because where he bit into the sod his teeth-print showed it. The millet-seed sifted out on one side—the ants told me that; the honey leaked out on the other—the flies told me that. I know all about your camel, but I hain't seen him."

Jim says:

"Go on, Mars Tom, hit's a mighty good tale, and powerful interestin'."

"That's all," Tom says.

"All?" says Jim, astonished.   "What 'come o' de camel?"

"I don't know."

"Mars Tom, don't de tale say?"

"No."

Jim puzzled a minute, then he says:

"Well!   Ef dat ain't de beatenes' tale ever *I* struck.   Jist gits to de place whah de intrust is gittin' red-hot, en down she breaks.   Why, Mars Tom, dey ain't no *sense* in a tale dat acts like dat.   Hain't you got no *idea* whether de man got de camel back er not?"

"No, I haven't."

I see myself there warn't no sense in the tale, to chop square off that way before it come to anything, but I warn't going to say so, because I could see Tom was souring up pretty fast over the way it flatted out and the way Jim had popped onto the weak place in it, and I don't think it's fair for everybody to pile onto a feller when he's down.   But Tom he whirls on me and says:

"What do *you* think of the tale?"

Of course, then, I had to come out and make a clean breast and say it did seem to me, too, same as it did to Jim, that as long as the tale stopped square in the middle and never got to no place, it really warn't worth the trouble of telling.

Tom's chin dropped on his breast, and 'stead of being mad, as I reckoned he'd be, to hear me scoff at his tale that way, he seemed to be only sad; and he says:

"Some people can see, and some can't—just as that man said. Let alone a camel, if a cyclone had gone by, *you* duffers wouldn't 'a' noticed the track."

I don't know what he meant by that, and he didn't say; it was just one of his irrulevances, I reckon—he was full of them, sometimes, when he was in a close place and couldn't see no other way out—but I didn't mind. We'd spotted the soft place in that tale sharp enough, he couldn't git away from that little fact. It graveled him like the nation, too, I reckon, much as he tried not to let on.

8: *The Disappearing Lake*

WE had an early breakfast in the morning, and set looking down on the desert, and the weather was ever so bammy and lovely, although we warn't high up. You have to come down lower and lower after sundown in the desert, because it cools off so fast; and so, by the time it is getting toward dawn, you are skimming along only a little ways above the sand.

We was watching the shadder of the balloon slide along the ground, and now and then gazing off across the desert to see if anything was stirring, and then down on the shadder again, when all of a sudden almost right under us we see a lot of men and camels laying scattered about, perfectly quiet, like they was asleep.

We shut off the power, and backed up and stood over them, and then we see that they was all dead. It give us the cold shivers. And it made us hush down, too, and talk low, like people at a funeral. We dropped down slow and stopped, and me and Tom clumb down and went among them. There was men, and women, and children. They was dried by the sun, and dark and shriveled and leathery, like the pictures of mummies you see in books. And yet they looked just as human, you wouldn't 'a' believed it; just like they was asleep.

Some of the people and animals was partly covered with sand, but most of them not, for the sand was thin there, and the bed was gravel and hard. Most of the clothes had rotted away; and when you took hold of a rag, it tore with a touch, like spider-web. Tom reckoned they had been laying there for years.

Some of the men had rusty guns by them, some had swords on and had shawl belts with long, silver-mounted pistols stuck in them. All the camels had their loads on yet, but the packs had busted or rotted and spilt the freight out on

the ground.   We didn't reckon the swords was
any good to the dead people any more, so we
took one apiece, and some pistols.   We took a
small box, too, because it was so handsome and
inlaid so fine; and then we wanted to bury the
people; but there warn't no way to do it that we
could think of, and nothing to do it with but
sand, and that would blow away again, of
course.

Then we mounted high and sailed away, and
pretty soon that black spot on the sand was out
of sight, and we wouldn't ever see them poor
people again in this world.   We wondered, and
reasoned, and tried to guess how they come to
be there, and how it all happened to them, but
we couldn't make it out.   First we thought
maybe they got lost, and wandered around and
about till their food and water give out and they
starved to death; but Tom said no wild animals
nor vultures hadn't meddled with them, and so
that guess wouldn't do.   So at last we give it up,
and judged we wouldn't think about it no more,
because it made us low-spirited.

Then we opened the box, and it had gems
and jewels in it, quite a pile, and some little
veils of the kind the dead women had on, with

fringes made out of curious gold money that we warn't acquainted with. We wondered if we better go and try to find them again and give it back; but Tom thought it over and said no, it was a country that was full of robbers, and they would come and steal it; and then the sin would be on us for putting the temptation in their way. So we went on; but I wished we had took all they had, so there wouldn't 'a' been no temptation at all left.

We had had two hours of that blazing weather down there, and was dreadful thirsty when we got aboard again. We went straight for the water, but it was spoiled and bitter, besides being pretty near hot enough to scald your mouth. We couldn't drink it. It was Mississippi River water, the best in the world, and we stirred up the mud in it to see if that would help, but no, the mud wasn't any better than the water.

Well, we hadn't been so very, very thirsty before, while we was interested in the lost people, but we was now, and as soon as we found we couldn't have a drink, we was more than thirty-five times as thirsty as we was a quarter of a minute before. Why, in a little while we wanted to hold our mouths open and pant like a dog.

Tom said to keep a sharp lookout, all around, everywheres, because we'd got to find an oasis or there warn't no telling what would happen. So we done it. We kept the glasses gliding around all the time, till our arms got so tired we couldn't hold them any more. Two hours— three hours—just gazing and gazing, and nothing but sand, sand, *sand,* and you could see the quivering heat-shimmer playing over it. Dear, dear, a body don't know what real misery is till he is thirsty all the way through and is certain he ain't ever going to come to any water any more. At last I couldn't stand it to look around on them baking plains; I laid down on the locker, and give it up.

But by and by Tom raised a whoop, and there she was! A lake, wide and shiny, with pa'm trees leaning over it asleep, and their shadders in the water just as soft and delicate as ever you see. I never see anything look so good. It was a long ways off, but that warn't anything to us; we just slapped on a hundred-mile gait, and calculated to be there in seven minutes; but she stayed the same old distance away, all the time;

we couldn't seem to gain on her; yes, sir, just as far, and shiny, and like a dream; but we couldn't get no nearer; and at last, all of a sudden, she was gone!

Tom's eyes took a spread, and he says:

"Boys, it was a *my*ridge!" Said it like he was glad. I didn't see nothing to be glad about. I says:

"Maybe. I don't care nothing about its name, the thing I want to know is, what's become of it?"

Jim was trembling all over, and so scared he couldn't speak, but he wanted to ask that question himself if he could 'a' done it. Tom says:

"What's *become* of it? Why, you see yourself it's gone."

"Yes, I know; but where's it gone *to?*"

He looked me over and says:

"Well, now, Huck Finn, where *would* it go to! Don't you know what a myridge is?"

"No, I don't. What is it?"

"It ain't anything but imagination. There ain't anything *to* it."

It warmed me up a little to hear him talk like that, and I says:

"What's the use you talking that kind of

stuff, Tom Sawyer? Didn't I see the lake?"

"Yes—you think you did."

"I don't think nothing about it, I *did* see it."

"I tell you you *didn't* see it either—because it warn't there to see."

It astonished Jim to hear him talk so, and he broke in and says, kind of pleading and distressed:

"Mars Tom, *please* don't say sich things in sich an awful time as dis. You ain't only reskin' yo' own self, but you's reskin' us—same way like Anna Nias en Siffira. De lake *wuz* dah—I seen it jis' as plain as I sees you en Huck dis minute."

I says:

"Why, he seen it himself! He was the very one that seen it first. *Now*, then!"

"Yes, Mars Tom, hit's so—you can't deny it. We all seen it, en dat *prove* it was dah."

"Proves it! *How* does it prove it?"

"Same way it does in de courts en everywheres, Mars Tom. One pusson might be drunk, or dreamy, or suthin', en he could be mistaken; en two might, maybe; but I tell you, sah, when three sees a thing, drunk or sober, it's *so*. Dey ain't no gettin' aroun' dat, en you knows it, Mars Tom."

"I don't know nothing of the kind. There used to be forty thousand million people that seen the sun move from one side of the sky to the other every day. Did that prove that the sun *done* it?"

" 'Course it did. En besides, dey warn't no 'casion to prove it. A body 'at's got any sense ain't gwine to doubt it. Dah she is now—a-sailin' thoo de sky, like she allays done."

Tom turned on me, then, and says:

"What do *you* say—is the sun standing still?"

"Tom Sawyer, what's the use to ask such a jackass question? Anybody that ain't blind can see it don't stand still."

"Well," he says, "I'm lost in the sky with no company but a passel of low-down animals that don't know no more than the head boss of a university did three or four hundred years ago."

It warn't fair play, and I let him know it. I says:

"Throwin' mud ain't arguin', Tom Sawyer."

"Oh, my goodness, oh, my goodness gracious, dah's de lake ag'in!" yelled Jim, just then.

"*Now,* Mars Tom, what you gwine to say?"

Yes, sir, there was the lake again, away yonder across the desert, perfectly plain, trees and all, just the same as it was before. I says:

"I reckon you're satisfied now, Tom Sawyer."

But he says, perfectly ca'm:

"Yes, satisfied there ain't no lake there."

Jim says:

"*Don't* talk so, Mars Tom—it sk'yers me to hear you. It's so hot, en you's so thirsty, dat you ain't in yo' right mine, Mars Tom. Oh, but don't she look good! 'clah I doan' know how I's gwine to wait tell we gits dah, I's *so* thirsty."

"Well, you'll have to wait; and it won't do you no good, either, because there ain't no lake there, I tell you."

I says:

"Jim, don't you take your eye off of it, and I won't, either."

" 'Deed I won't; en bless you, honey, I couldn't ef I wanted to."

We went a-tearing along toward it, piling the miles behind us like nothing, but never gaining an inch on it—and all of a sudden it was gone again! Jim staggered, and 'most fell down.

When he got his breath he says, gasping like a fish:

"Mars Tom, hit's a *ghos'*, dat's what it is, en I hopes to goodness we ain't gwine to see it no mo'. Dey's *been* a lake, en suthin's happened, en de lake's dead, en we's seen its ghos'; we's seen it twiste, en dat's proof. De desert's ha'nted, it's ha'nted, sho; oh, Mars Tom, le's git outen it; I'd ruther die den have de night ketch us in it ag'in en de ghos' er dat lake come a-mournin' aroun' us en we asleep en doan' know de danger we's in."

"Ghost, you gander! It ain't anything but air and heat and thirstiness pasted together by a person's imagination. If I—gimme the glass!"

He grabbed it and begun to gaze off to the right.

"It's a flock of birds," he says. "It's getting toward sundown, and they're making a bee-line across our track for somewheres. They mean business—maybe they're going for food or water, or both. Let her go to starboard!—Port your hellum! Hard down! There—ease up —steady, as you go."

We shut down some of the power, so as not to outspeed them, and took out after them. We went skimming along a quarter of a mile behind them, and when we had followed them an hour and a half and was getting pretty discouraged, and was thirsty clean to unendurableness, Tom says:

"Take the glass, one of you, and see what that is, away ahead of the birds."

Jim got the first glimpse, and slumped down on the locker sick. He was 'most crying, and says:

"She's dah ag'in, Mars Tom, she's dah ag'in, en I knows I's gwine to die, 'case when a body sees a ghos' de third time, dat's what it means. I wisht I'd never come in dis balloon, dat I does."

He wouldn't look no more, and what he said made me afraid, too, because I knowed it was true, for that has always been the way with ghosts; so then I wouldn't look any more, either. Both of us begged Tom to turn off and go some other way, but he wouldn't, and said we was ignorant superstitious blatherskites. Yes, and he'll git come up with, one of these days, I says to myself, insulting ghosts that way. They'll stand it for a while, maybe, but they won't stand it always, for anybody that knows about ghosts

knows how easy they are hurt, and how revenge-
ful they are.

So we was all quiet and still, Jim and me
being scared, and Tom busy. By and by Tom
fetched the balloon to a standstill, and says:

"*Now* get up and look, you sapheads."

We done it, and there was the sure-enough
water right under us!—clear, and blue, and
cool, and deep, and wavy with the breeze, the
loveliest sight that ever was. And all about it
was grassy banks, and flowers, and shady groves
of big trees, looped together with vines, and all
looking so peaceful and comfortable—enough
to make a body cry, it was so beautiful.

Jim *did* cry, and rip and dance and carry on,
he was so thankful and out of his mind for joy.
It was my watch, so I had to stay by the works,
but Tom and Jim clumb down and drunk a
barrel apiece, and fetched me up a lot, and I've
tasted a many a good thing in my life, but nothing that ever begun with that water.

Then they went down and had a swim, and
then Tom came up and spelled me, and me and
Jim had a swim, and then Jim spelled Tom, and
me and Tom had a foot-race and a boxing-mill,

Then we went down and had a swim

and I don't reckon I ever had such a good time in my life. It warn't so very hot, because it was close on to evening, and we hadn't any clothes on, anyway. Clothes is well enough in school, and in towns, and at balls, too, but there ain't no sense in them when there ain't no civilization nor other kinds of bothers and fussiness around.

"Lions a-comin'!—lions! Quick, Mars Tom! Jump for yo' life, Huck!"

Oh, and didn't we! We never stopped for clothes, but waltzed up the ladder just so. Jim lost his head straight off—he always done it whenever he got excited and scared; and so now, 'stead of just easing the ladder up from the ground a little, so the animals couldn't reach it, he turned on a raft of power, and we went whizzing up and was dangling in the sky before he got his wits together and seen what a foolish thing he was doing. Then he stopped her, but he had clean forgot what to do next; so there we was, so high that the lions looked like pups, and we was drifting off on the wind.

But Tom he shinned up and went for the works and begun to slant her down, and back toward the lake, where the animals was gathering like a camp-meeting, and I judged he had lost *his* head, too; for he knowed I was too scared to climb, and did he want to dump me among the tigers and things?

But no, his head was level; he knowed what he was about. He swooped down to within thirty or forty feet of the lake, and stopped right over the center, and sung out:

"Leggo, and drop!"

I done it, and shot down, feet first, and seemed to go about a mile toward the bottom; and when I come up, he says:

"Now lay on your back and float till you're rested and got your pluck back, then I'll dip the ladder in the water and you can climb aboard."

I done it. Now that was ever so smart in Tom, because if he had started off somewheres else to drop down on the sand, the menagerie would 'a' come along, too, and might 'a' kept us hunting a safe place till I got tuckered out and fell.

And all this time the lions and tigers was sorting out the clothes, and trying to divide them up so there would be some for all, but there was a misunderstanding about it somewheres, on account of some of them trying to

hog more than their share; so there was another
insurrection, and you never see anything like it
in the world.   There must 'a' been fifty of them,
all mixed up together, snorting and roaring and
snapping and biting and tearing, legs and tails
in the air, and you couldn't tell which was
which, and the sand and fur a-flying.   And
when they got done, some was dead, and some
was limping off crippled, and the rest was setting around on the battle-field, some of them
licking their sore places and the others looking
up at us and seemed to be kind of inviting us to
come down and have some fun, but which we
didn't want any.

As for the clothes, they warn't any, any more.
Every last rag of them was inside of the animals;
and not agreeing with them very well, I don't
reckon, for there was considerable many brass
buttons on them, and there was knives in the
pockets too, and smoking-tobacco, and nails and
chalk and marbles and fishhooks and things.
But I wasn't caring.   All that was bothering me
was, that all we had now was the professor's
clothes, a big enough assortment, but not suit-
able to go into company with, if we came across
any, because the britches was as long as tunnels,

and the coats and things according.   Still, there
was everything a tailor needed, and Jim was a
kind of jack-legged tailor, and he allowed he
could soon trim a suit or two down for us that
would answer.

9: *Tom Discourses on the Desert*

STILL, we thought we would drop down there a minute, but on another errand. Most of the professor's cargo of food was put up in cans, in the new way that somebody had just invented; the rest was fresh. When you fetch Missouri beefsteak to the Great Sahara, you want to be particular and stay up in the coolish weather. So we reckoned we would drop down into the lion market and see how we could make out there.

We hauled in the ladder and dropped down till we was just above the reach of the animals, then we let down a rope with a slip-knot in it and hauled up a dead lion, a small tender one, then yanked up a cub tiger. We had to keep the congregation off with the revolver, or they would 'a' took a hand in the proceedings and helped.

We carved off a supply from both, and saved the skins, and hove the rest overboard. Then we baited some of the professor's hooks with the fresh meat and went a-fishing. We stood over the lake just a convenient distance above the water, and catched a lot of the nicest fish you ever see. It was a most amazing good supper we had; lion steak, tiger steak, fried fish, and hot corn-pone. I don't want nothing better than that.

We had some fruit to finish off with. We got it out of the top of a monstrous tall tree. It was a very slim tree that hadn't a branch on it from the bottom plumb to the top, and there it bursted out like a feather duster. It was a pa'm tree, of course; anybody knows a pa'm tree the minute he see it, by the pictures. We went for cocoanuts in this one, but there warn't none. There was only big loose bunches of things like oversized grapes, and Tom allowed they was dates, because he said they answered the description in the *Arabian Nights* and the other books. Of course they mightn't be, and they might be poison; so we had to wait a spell, and watch and see if the birds et them. They done it; so we done it, too, and they was most amazing good.

By this time monstrous big birds begun to come and settle on the dead animals. They were plucky creturs; they would tackle one end of a lion that was being gnawed at the other end by another lion. If the lion drove the bird away, it didn't do no good; he was back again the minute the lion was busy.

The big birds come out of every part of the sky—you could make them out with the glass while they was still so far away you couldn't see them with your naked eye. Tom said the birds didn't find out the meat was there by the smell; they had to find it out by seeing it. Oh, but ain't that an eye for you! Tom said at the distance of five mile a patch of dead lions couldn't look any bigger than a person's finger-nail, and he couldn't imagine how the birds could notice such a little thing so far off.

It was strange and unnatural to see lion eat lion, and we thought maybe they warn't kin.

But Jim said that didn't make no difference. He said a hog was fond of her own children, and so was a spider, and he reckoned maybe a lion was pretty near as unprincipled, though maybe not quite. He thought likely a lion wouldn't eat his own father, if he knowed which was him, but reckoned he would eat his brother-in-law if he was uncommon hungry, and eat his mother-in-law any time. But *reckoning* don't settle nothing. You can reckon till the cows come home, but that don't fetch you to no decision. So we give it up and let it drop.

Generly it was very still in the desert nights, but this time there was music. A lot of other animals come to dinner; sneaking yelpers that Tom allowed was jackals, and roached-backed ones that he said was hyenas; and all the whole biling of them kept up a racket all the time. They made a picture in the moonlight that was more different than any picture I ever see. We had a line out and made fast to the top of a tree, and didn't stand no watch, but all turned in and slept; but I was up two or three times to look down at the animals and hear the music. It was like having a front seat at a menagerie for nothing, which I hadn't ever had before, and so it seemed foolish to sleep and not make the most of it; I mightn't ever have such a chance again.

We went a-fishing again in the early dawn, and then lazied around all day in the deep shade on an island, taking turn about to watch and see that none of the animals come a-snooping around there after erronorts for dinner. We was going to leave the next day, but couldn't, it was too lovely.

The day after, when we rose up toward the sky and sailed off eastward, we looked back and watched that place till it warn't nothing but just a speck in the desert, and I tell you it was like saying good-by to a friend that you ain't ever going to see any more.

Jim was thinking to himself, and at last he says: "Mars Tom, we's mos' to de end er de desert now, I speck."

"Why?"

"Well, hit stan' to reason we is. You knows how long we's been a-skimmin' over it. Mus' be mos' out o' san'. Hit's a wonder to me dat it's hilt out as long as it has."

"Shucks, there's plenty sand, you needn't worry."

"Oh, I ain't a-worryin', Mars Tom, only wonderin', dat's all. De Lord's got plenty san', I ain't doubtin' dat; but nemmine, He ain't gwyne to *was'e* it jist on dat account; en I allows dat dis desert's plenty big enough now, jist de way she is, en you can't spread her out no mo' 'dout was'in' san'."

"Oh, go 'long! we ain't much more than fairly *started* across this desert yet. The United States is a pretty big country, ain't it? Ain't it, Huck?"

"Yes," I says, "there ain't no bigger one, I don't reckon."

"Well," he says, "this desert is about the shape of the United States, and if you was to lay it down on top of the United States, it would cover the land of the free out of sight like a blanket. There'd be a little corner sticking out, up at Maine and away up northwest, and Florida sticking out like a turtle's tail, and that's all. We've took California away from the Mexicans two or three years ago, so that part of the Pacific coast is ours now, and if you laid the Great Sahara down with her edge on the Pacific, she would cover the United States and stick out

past New York six hundred miles into the Atlantic Ocean."

I says:

"Good land! have you got the documents for
that, Tom Sawyer?"

"Yes, and they're right here, and I've been
studying them. You can look for yourself.
From New York to the Pacific is 2,600 miles.
From one end of the Great Desert to the other is
3,200. The United States contains 3,600,000
square miles, the desert contains 4,162,000.
With the desert's bulk you could cover up every
last inch of the United States, and in under,
where the edges projected out, you could tuck
England, Scotland, Ireland, France, Denmark,
and all Germany. Yes, sir, you could hide the
home of the brave and all of them countries
clean out of sight under the Great Sahara, and
you would still have 2,000 square miles of sand
left."

"Well," I says, "it clean beats me. Why,
Tom, it shows that the Lord took as much pains
makin' this desert as makin' the United States
and all them other countries."

Jim says: "Huck, dat don' stan' to reason. I
reckon dis desert wa'n't made at all. Now you

take en look at it like dis—you look at it, and see ef I's right. What's a desert good for? 'Tain't good for nuthin'. Dey ain't no way to make it pay. Hain't dat so, Huck?"

"Yes, I reckon."

"Hain't it so, Mars Tom?"

"I guess so. Go on."

"Ef a thing ain't no good, it's made in vain, ain't it?"

"Yes."

"*Now*, den! Do de Lord make anything in vain? You answer me dat."

"Well—no, He don't."

"Den how come He make a desert?"

"Well, go on. How *did* He come to make it?"

"Mars Tom, *I* b'lieve it uz jes like when you's buildin' a house; dey's allays a lot o' truck en rubbish lef' over. What does you do wid it? Doan' you take en k'yart it off en dump it into a ole vacant back lot? 'Course. Now, den, it's my opinion hit was jest like dat—dat de Great Sahara warn't made at all, she jes' *happen'*."

I said it was a real good argument, and I believed it was the best one Jim ever made. Tom he said the same, but said the trouble about arguments is, they ain't nothing but *theories*, after all, and theories don't prove nothing, they only give you a place to rest on, a spell, when you are tuckered out butting around and around trying to find out something there ain't no way *to* find out. And he says:

"There's another trouble about theories: there's always a hole in them somewhere's, sure, if you look close enough. It's just so with this one of Jim's. Look what billions and billions of stars there is. How does it come that there was just exactly enough star-stuff, and none left over? How does it come there ain't no sand-pile up there?"

But Jim was fixed for him and says:

"What's de Milky Way?—dat's what *I* want to know. What's de Milky Way? Answer me dat!"

In my opinion it was just a sockdologer. It's only an opinion, it's only *my* opinion and others may think different; but I said it then and I stand to it now—it was a sockdologer. And moreover, besides, it landed Tom Sawyer. He couldn't say a word. He had that stunned look of a person that's been shot in the back with a kag of nails. All he said was, as for people like me and Jim, he'd just as soon have intellectual intercourse with a catfish. But anybody can say that—and I notice they always do when somebody has fetched them a lifter. Tom Sawyer was tired of that end of the subject.

So we got back to talking about the size of the desert again, and the more we compared it with this and that and t'other thing, the more nobler and bigger and grander it got to look right along. And so, hunting among the figgers, Tom found, by and by, that it was just the same size as the Empire of China. Then he showed us the spread the Empire of China made on the map, and the room she took up in the world. Well, it was wonderful to think of, and I says:

"Why, I've heard talk about this desert plenty of times, but *I* never knowed before how important she was."

Then Tom says:

"Important! Sahara important! That's just the way with some people. If a thing's big, it's important. That's all the sense they've got. All they can see is *size*. Why, look at England. It's the most important country in the world; and yet you could put it in China's vest-pocket; and not only that, but you'd have the dickens's own time to find it again the next time you wanted it.   And look at Russia.   It spreads all around and everywhere, and yet ain't no more important in this world than Rhode Island is, and hasn't got half as much in it that's worth saving."

Away off now we see a little hill, a-standing up just on the edge of the world.   Tom broke off his talk, and reached for a glass very much excited, and took a look, and says:

"That's it—it's the one I've been looking for, sure.   If I'm right, it's the one the dervish took the man into and showed him all the treasures."

So we begun to gaze, and he begun to tell about it out of the *Arabian Nights*.

10: *The Treasure-Hill*

TOM said it happened like this:

A dervish was stumping it along through the
desert, on foot, one blazing hot day, and he had
come a thousand miles and was pretty poor, and
hungry, and ornery and tired, and along about
where we are now he run across a camel-driver
with a hundred camels, and asked him for some
a'ms. But the camel-driver he asked to be ex-
cused. The dervish said:

"Don't you own these camels?"

"Yes, they're mine."

"Are you in debt?"

"Who—me? No."

"Well, a man that owns a hundred camels and ain't in debt is rich—and not only rich, but very rich. Ain't it so?"

The camel-driver owned up that it was so. Then the dervish says:

"God has made you rich, and He has made me poor. He has His reasons, and they are wise, blessed be His name. But He has willed that His rich shall help His poor, and you have turned away from me, your brother, in my need, and He will remember this, and you will lose by it."

That made the camel-driver feel shaky, but all the same he was born hoggish after money and didn't like to let go a cent; so he begun to whine and explain, and said times was hard, and although he had took a full freight down to Balsora and got a fat rate for it, he couldn't git no return freight, and so he warn't making no great things out of his trip. So the dervish starts along again, and says:

"All right, if you want to take the risk; but I reckon you've made a mistake this time, and missed a chance."

Of course the camel-driver wanted to know what kind of a chance he had missed, because

maybe there was money in it; so he run after the
dervish, and begged him so hard and earnest to
take pity on him that at last the dervish gave in,
and says:

"Do you see that hill yonder?   Well, in that
hill is all the treasures of the earth, and I was
looking around for a man with a particular
good kind heart and a noble, generous disposi-
tion, because if I could find just that man, I've
got a kind of a salve I could put on his eyes and
he could see the treasures and get them out."

So then the camel-driver was in a sweat; and
he cried, and begged, and took on, and went
down on his knees, and said he was just that
kind of a man, and said he could fetch a thousand people that would say he warn't ever de-
scribed so exact before.

"Well, then," says the dervish, "all right.   If
we load the hundred camels, can I have half of
them?"

The driver was so glad he couldn't hardly
hold in, and says:

"Now you're shouting."

So they shook hands on the bargain, and the
dervish got out his box and rubbed the salve on
the driver's right eye, and the hill opened and

he went in, and there, sure enough, was piles and piles of gold and jewels sparkling like all the stars in heaven had fell down.

So him and the dervish laid into it, and they loaded every camel till he couldn't carry no more; then they said good-by, and each of them started off with his fifty. But pretty soon the camel-driver come a-running and overtook the dervish and says:

"You ain't in society, you know, and you don't really need all you've got. Won't you be good, and let me have ten of your camels?"

"Well," the dervish says, "I don't know but what you say is reasonable enough."

So he done it, and they separated, and the dervish started off again with his forty. But pretty soon here comes the camel-driver bawling after him again, and whines and slobbers around and begs another ten off of him, saying thirty camel-loads of treasures was enough to see a dervish through, because they live very simple, you know, and don't keep house, but board around and give their note.

But that warn't the end yet. That ornery hound kept coming and coming till he had begged back all the camels and had the whole hundred. Then he was satisfied, and ever so grateful, and said he wouldn't ever forgit the dervish as long as he lived, and nobody hadn't been so good to him before, and liberal. So they shook hands good-by, and separated and started off again.

But do you know, it warn't ten minutes till the camel-driver was unsatisfied again—he was the low-downest reptile in seven counties—and he come a-running again. And this time the thing he wanted was to get the dervish to rub some of the salve on his other eye.

"Why?" said the dervish.

"Oh, you know," says the driver.

"Know what?"

"Well, you can't fool me," says the driver. "You're trying to keep back something from me, you know it mighty well. You know, I reckon, that if I had the salve on the other eye I could see a lot more things that's valuable. Come—please put it on."

The dervish says:

"I wasn't keeping anything back from you. I don't mind telling you what would happen if I put it on. You'd never see again. You'd be stone-blind the rest of your days."

But do you know that beat wouldn't believe
him. No, he begged and begged, and whined
and cried, till at last the dervish opened his box
and told him to put it on, if he wanted to. So
the man done it, and, sure enough, he was as
blind as a bat in a minute.

Then the dervish laughed at him and mocked
at him and made fun of him; and says:

"Good-by—a man that's blind hain't got no
use for jewelry."

And he cleared out with the hundred camels,
and left that man to wander around poor and
miserable and friendless the rest of his days in
the desert.

Jim said he'd bet it was a lesson to him.

"Yes," Tom says, "and like a considerable
many lessons a body gets. They ain't no account, because the thing don't ever happen the
same way again—and can't. The time Hen
Scovil fell down the chimbly and crippled his
back for life, everybody said it would be a lesson
to him. What kind of a lesson? How was he
going to use it? He couldn't climb chimblies
no more, and he hadn't no more backs to
break."

"All de same, Mars Tom, dey *is* sich a thing as

learnin' by expe'ence. De Good Book say de burnt chile shun de fire."

"Well, I ain't denying that a thing's a lesson if it's a thing that can happen twice just the same way. There's lots of such things, and *they* educate a person, that's what Uncle Abner always said; but there's forty *million* lots of the other kind—the kind that don't happen the same way twice—and they ain't no real use, they ain't no more instructive than the smallpox. When you've got it, it ain't no good to find out you ought to been vaccinated, and it ain't no good to git vaccinated afterward, because the smallpox don't come but once. But, on the other hand, Uncle Abner said that the person that had took a bull by the tail once had learnt sixty or seventy times as much as a person that hadn't, and said a person that started in to carry a cat home by the tail was gitting knowledge that was always going to be useful to him, and warn't ever going to grow dim or doubtful. But I can tell you, Jim, Uncle Abner was down on them people that's all the time trying to dig a lesson out of everything that happens, no matter whether—"

But Jim was asleep. Tom looked kind of ashamed, because you know a person always

feels bad when he is talking uncommon fine and
thinks the other person is admiring, and that
other person goes to sleep that way. Of course
he oughtn't to go to sleep, because it's shabby;
but the finer a person talks the certainer it is to
make you sleep, and so when you come to look
at it it ain't nobody's fault in particular; both of
them's to blame.

Jim begun to snore—soft and blubbery at
first, then a long rasp, then a stronger one, then
a half a dozen horrible ones, like the last water
sucking down the plug-hole of a bathtub, then
the same with more power to it, and some big
coughs and snorts flung in, the way a cow does
that is choking to death; and when the person
has got to that point he is at his level best, and
can wake up a man that is in the next block with
a dipperful of loddanum in him, but can't wake
himself up although all that awful noise of his'n
ain't but three inches from his own ears. And
that is the curiousest thing in the world, seems
to me. But you rake a match to light the
candle, and that little bit of a noise will fetch
him. I wish I knowed what was the reason of
that, but there don't seem to be no way to find
out. Now there was Jim alarming the whole

desert, and yanking the animals out, for miles
and miles around, to see what in the nation was
going on up there; there warn't nobody nor
nothing that was as close to the noise as *he* was,
and yet he was the only cretur that wasn't disturbed by it. We yelled at him and whooped at
him, it never done no good; but the first time
there come a little wee noise that wasn't of a
usual kind, it woke him up. No, sir, I've
thought it all over, and so has Tom, and there
ain't no way to find out why a snorer can't hear
himself snore.

Jim said he hadn't been asleep; he just shut
his eyes so he could listen better.

Tom said nobody warn't accusing him.

That made him look like he wished he hadn't
said anything. And he wanted to git away from
the subject, I reckon, because he begun to abuse
the camel-driver, just the way a person does
when he has got catched in something and wants
to take it out of somebody else. He let into the
camel-driver the hardest he knowed how, and I
had to agree with him; and he praised up the
dervish the highest he could, and I had to agree
with him there, too. But Tom says:

"I ain't so sure. You call that dervish so

dreadful liberal and good and unselfish, but I don't quite see it.   He didn't hunt up another poor dervish, did he?   No, he didn't.   If he was so unselfish, why didn't he go in there himself and take a pocketful of jewels and go along and be satisfied?   No, sir, the person he was hunting for was a man with a hundred camels.   He wanted to get away with all the treasure he could."

"Why, Mars Tom, he was willin' to divide, fair and square; he only struck for fifty camels."

"Because he knowed how he was going to git all of them by and by."

"Mars Tom, he *tole* de man de truck would make him bline."

"Yes, because he knowed the man's character. It was just the kind of a man he was hunting for—a man that never believes in anybody's word or anybody's honorableness, because he ain't got none of his own.   I reckon there's lots of people like that dervish.   They swindle, right and left, but they always make the other person *seem* to swindle himself.   They keep inside of the letter of the law all the time, and there ain't no way to git hold of them.   *They* don't put the salve on—oh, no, that would be sin; but they know how to fool *you* into putting it on, then it's you that blinds yourself. I reckon the dervish and the camel-driver was just a pair—a fine, smart, brainy rascal, and a dull, coarse, ignorant one, but both of them rascals, just the same."

"Mars Tom, does you reckon dey's any o' dat kind o' salve in de worl' now?"

"Yes, Uncle Abner says there is. He says they've got it in New York, and they put it on country people's eyes and show them all the railroads in the world, and they go in and git them, and then when they rub the salve on the other eye the other man bids them good-by and goes off with their railroads. Here's the treasure-hill now. Lower away!"

We landed, but it warn't as interesting as I thought it was going to be, because we couldn't find the place where they went in to git the treasure. Still, it was plenty interesting enough, just to see the mere hill itself where such a wonderful thing happened. Jim said he wouldn't 'a' missed it for three dollars, and I felt the same way.

And to me and Jim, as wonderful a thing as any was the way Tom could come into a strange

big country like this and go straight and find a
little hump like that and tell it in a minute from
a million other humps that was almost just like
it, and nothing to help him but only his own
learning and his own natural smartness.   We
talked and talked it over together, but couldn't
make out how he done it.   He had the best head
on him I ever see; and all he lacked was age to
make a name for himself equal to Captain Kidd
or George Washington.   I bet you it would 'a'
crowded either of *them* to find that hill, with all
their gifts, but it warn't nothing to Tom Sawyer; he went across Sahara and put his finger on
it as easy as you could pick a darky out of a
bunch of angels.

We found a pond of salt-water close by and
scraped up a raft of salt around the edges, and
loaded up the lion's skin and the tiger's so as
they would keep till Jim could tan them.

11: *The Sandstorm*

WE went a-fooling along for a day or two, and
then just as the full moon was touching the
ground on the other side of the desert, we see a
string of little black figgers moving across its big
silver face. You could see them as plain as if
they was painted on the moon with ink. It was
another caravan. We cooled down our speed
and tagged along after it, just to have company,
though it warn't going our way. It was a rat-
tler, that caravan, and a most bully sight to look
at next morning when the sun come a-streaming
across the desert and flung the long shadders of
the camels on the gold sand like a thousand

grand-daddy-long-legses marching in procession. We never went very near it, because we knowed better now than to act like that and scare people's camels and break up their caravans. It was the gayest outfit you ever see, for rich clothes and nobby style. Some of the chiefs rode on dromedaries, the first we ever see, and very tall, and they go plunging along like they was on stilts, and they rock the man that is on them pretty violent and churn up his dinner considerable, I bet you, but they make noble good time, and a camel ain't nowheres with them for speed.

The caravan camped, during the middle part of the day, and then started again about the middle of the afternoon. Before long the sun begun to look very curious. First it kind of turned to brass, and then to copper, and after that it begun to look like a blood-red ball, and the air got hot and close, and pretty soon all the sky in the west darkened up and looked thick and foggy, but fiery and dreadful—like it looks through a piece of red glass, you know. We looked down and see a big confusion going on in the caravan, and a rushing every which way like they was scared; and then they all flopped down flat in the sand and laid there perfectly still.

Pretty soon we see something coming that stood up like an amazing wide wall, and reached from the desert up into the sky and hid the sun, and it was coming like the nation, too.   Then a little faint breeze struck us, and then it come harder, and grains of sand begun to sift against our faces and sting like fire, and Tom sung out:

"It's a sandstorm—turn your backs to it!"

We done it; and in another minute it was blowing a gale, and the sand beat against us by the shovelful, and the air was so thick with it we couldn't see a thing.   In five minutes the boat was level full, and we was setting on the lockers buried up to the chin in sand, and only our heads out and could hardly breathe.

Then the storm thinned, and we see that monstrous wall go a-sailing off across the desert, awful to look at, I tell you.   We dug ourselves out and looked down, and where the caravan was before there wasn't anything but just the sand ocean now, and all still and quiet.   All them people and camels was smothered and dead and buried—buried under ten foot of sand, we reckoned, and Tom allowed it might be years before the wind uncovered them, and

The sand beat against us by the shovelful

all that time their friends wouldn't ever know what become of that caravan. Tom said:

"*Now* we know what it was that happened to the people we got the swords and pistols from."

Yes, sir, that was just it. It was as plain as day now. They got buried in a sandstorm, and the wild animals couldn't get at them, and the wind never uncovered them again until they was dried to leather and warn't fit to eat. It seemed to me we had felt as sorry for them poor people as a person could for anybody, and as mournful, too, but we was mistaken; this last caravan's death went harder with us, a good deal harder. You see, the others was total strangers, and we never got to feeling acquainted with them at all, except, maybe, a little with the man that was watching the girl, but it was different with this last caravan. We was huvvering around them a whole night and 'most a whole day, and had got to feeling real friendly with them, and acquainted. I have found out that there ain't no surer way to find out whether you like people or hate them than to travel with them. Just so with these. We kind of liked them from the start, and traveling with them put on the finisher. The longer we traveled with them, and

the more we got used to their ways, the better
and better we liked them, and the gladder and
gladder we was that we run across them. We
had come to know some of them so well that we
called them by name when we was talking about
them, and soon got so familiar and sociable that
we even dropped the Miss and Mister and just
used their plain names without any handle, and
it did not seem unpolite, but just the right
thing. Of course, it wasn't their own names,
but names we give them. There was Mr. Elex-
ander Robinson and Miss Adaline Robinson,
and Colonel Jacob McDougal and Miss Harryet
McDougal, and Judge Jeremiah Butler and
young Bushrod Butler, and these was big chiefs
mostly that wore splendid great turbans and
simmeters, and dressed like the Grand Mogul,
and their families. But as soon as we come to
know them good, and like them very much, it
warn't Mister, nor Judge, nor nothing, any
more, but only Elleck, and Addy, and Jake, and
Hattie, and Jerry, and Buck, and so on.

And you know the more you join in with
people in their joys and their sorrows, the more
nearer and dearer they come to be to you. Now
we warn't cold and indifferent, the way most

travelers is, we was right down friendly and sociable, and took a chance in everything that was
going, and the caravan could depend on us to be
on hand every time, it didn't make no difference
what it was.

When they camped, we camped right over
them, ten or twelve hundred feet up in the air.
When they et a meal, we et ourn, and it made it
ever so much homeliker to have their company.
When they had a wedding that night, and Buck
and Addy got married, we got ourselves up in
the very starchiest of the professor's duds for the
blow-out, and when they danced we jined in
and shook a foot up there.

But it is sorrow and trouble that brings you
the nearest, and it was a funeral that done it
with us. It was next morning, just in the still
dawn. We didn't know the diseased, and he
warn't in our set, but that never made no difference; he belonged to the caravan, and that was
enough, and there warn't no more sincerer tears
shed over him than the ones we dripped on him
from up there eleven hundred foot on high.

Yes, parting with this caravan was much more
bitterer than it was to part with them others,
which was comparative strangers, and been

dead so long, anyway. We had knowed these in their lives and was fond of them, too, and now to have death snatch them from right before our faces while we was looking, and leave us so lonesome and friendless in the middle of that big desert, it did hurt so, and we wished we mightn't ever make any more friends on that voyage if we was going to lose them again like that.

We couldn't keep from talking about them, and they was all the time coming up in our memory, and looking just the way they looked when we was all alive and happy together. We could see the line marching, and the shiny spearheads a-winking in the sun; we could see the dromedaries lumbering along; we could see the wedding and the funeral; and more oftener than anything else we could see them praying, because they don't allow nothing to prevent that; whenever the call come, several times a day, they would stop right there, and stand up and face to the east, and lift back their heads, and spread out their arms and begin, and four or five times they would go down on their knees, and then fall forward and touch their forehead to the ground.

Well, it warn't good to go on talking about them, lovely as they was in their life, and dear to us in their life and death both, because it didn't do no good, and made us too downhearted. Jim allowed he was going to live as good a life as he could, so he could see them again in a better world; and Tom kept still and didn't tell him they was only Mohammedans; it warn't no use to disappoint him, he was feeling bad enough just as it was.

When we woke up next morning we was feeling a little cheerfuler, and had had a most powerful good sleep, because sand is the comfortablest bed there is, and I don't see why people that can afford it don't have it more. And it's terrible good ballast, too; I never see the balloon so steady before.

Tom allowed we had twenty tons of it, and wondered what we better do with it; it was good sand, and it didn't seem good sense to throw it away. Jim says:

"Mars Tom, can't we tote it back home en sell it? How long'll it take?"

"Depends on the way we go."

"Well, sah, she's wuth a quarter of a dollar a load at home, en I reckon we's got as much as twenty loads, hain't we?   How much would dat be?"

"Five dollars."

"By jings, Mars Tom, le's shove for home right on de spot!   Hit's more'n a dollar en a half apiece, hain't it?"

"Yes."

"Well, ef dat ain't makin' money de easiest ever *I* struck!   She jes' rained in—never cos' us a lick o' work.   Le's mosey right along, Mars Tom."

But Tom was thinking and ciphering away so busy and excited he never heard him.   Pretty soon he says:

"Five dollars—sho!   Look here, this sand's worth—worth—why, it's worth no end of money."

"How is dat, Mars Tom?   Go on, honey, go on!"

"Well, the minute people knows it's genuwyne sand from the genuwyne Desert of Sahara, they'll just be in a perfect state of mind to git hold of some of it to keep on the what-not in a vial with a label on it for a curiosity.   All we got to do is to put it up in vials and float around all over the United States and peddle them out at ten cents apiece. We've got all of ten thousand dollars' worth of sand in this boat."

Me and Jim went all to pieces with joy, and begun to shout whoopjamboreehoo, and Tom says:

"And we can keep on coming back and fetching sand, and coming back and fetching more sand, and just keep it a-going till we've carted this whole desert over there and sold it out; and there ain't ever going to be any opposition, either, because we'll take out a patent."

"My goodness," I says, "we'll be as rich as Creosote, won't we, Tom?"

"Yes—Creesus, you mean. Why, that dervish was hunting in that little hill for the treasures of the earth, and didn't know he was walking over the real ones for a thousand miles. He was blinder than he made the driver."

"Mars Tom, how much is we gwyne to be worth?"

"Well, I don't know yet. It's got to be ciphered, and it ain't the easiest job to do, either, because it's over four million square miles of sand at ten cents a vial."

Jim was awful excited, but this faded it out considerable, and he shook his head and says:

"Mars Tom, we can't 'ford all dem vials—a king couldn't. We better not try to take de whole desert, Mars Tom, de vials gwyne to bust us, sho'."

Tom's excitement died out, too, now, and I reckoned it was on account of the vials, but it wasn't. He set there thinking, and got bluer and bluer, and at last he says:

"Boys, it won't work; we got to give it up."

"Why, Tom?"

"On account of the duties."

I couldn't make nothing out of that, neither could Jim. I says:

"What *is* our duty, Tom? Because if we can't git around it, why can't we just *do* it? People often has to."

But he says:

"Oh, it ain't that kind of duty. The kind I mean is a tax. Whenever you strike a frontier —that's the border of a country, you know— you find a custom-house there, and the gov'ment officers comes and rummages among your things and charges a big tax, which they call a duty because it's their duty to bust you if they can, and if you don't pay the duty they'll hog your sand. They call it confiscating, but

that don't deceive nobody, it's just hogging, and
that's all it is.   Now if we try to carry this sand
home the way we're pointed now, we got to
climb fences till we git tired—just frontier after
frontier—Egypt, Arabia, Hindustan, and so on,
and they'll all whack on a duty, and so you see,
easy enough, we *can't* go *that* road."

"Why, Tom," I says, "we can sail right over
their old frontiers; how are *they* going to stop
us?"

He looked sorrowful at me, and says, very
grave: "Huck Finn, do you think that would
be honest?"

I hate them kind of interruptions. I never
said nothing, and he went on:

"Well, we're shut off the other way, too.   If
we go back the way we've come, there's the New
York custom-house, and that is worse than all of
them others put together, on account of the
kind of cargo we've got."

"Why?"

"Well, they can't raise Sahara sand in
America, of course, and when they can't raise
a thing there, the duty is fourteen hundred
thousand per cent on it if you try to fetch it in
from where they do raise it."

"There ain't no sense in that, Tom Sawyer."

"Who said there *was?* What do you talk to me like that for, Huck Finn? You wait till I say a thing's got sense in it before you go to accusing me of saying it."

"All right, consider me crying about it, and sorry. Go on."

Jim says:

"Mars Tom, do dey jam dat duty onto everything we can't raise in America, en don't make no 'stinction 'twix' anything?"

"Yes, that's what they do."

"Mars Tom, ain't de blessin' o' de Lord de mos' valuable thing dey is?"

"Yes, it is."

"Don't de preacher stan' up in de pulpit en call it down on de people?"

"Yes."

"Whah do it come from?"

"From heaven."

"Yassir! you's jes' right, 'deed you is, honey —it come from heaven, en dat's a foreign country. *Now,* den! do dey put a tax on dat blessin'?"

"No, they don't."

" 'Course dey don't; en so it stan' to reason dat you's mistaken, Mars Tom. Dey wouldn't put de tax on po' truck like san', dat everybody ain't 'bleeged to have, en leave it off'n de bes' thing dey is, which nobody can't git along wid-out."

Tom Sawyer was stumped; he see Jim had got him where he couldn't budge. He tried to wig-gle out by saying they had *forgot* to put on that tax, but they'd be sure to remember about it, next session of Congress, and then they'd put it on, but that was a poor lame come-off, and he knowed it. He said there warn't nothing for-eign that warn't taxed but just that one, and so they couldn't be consistent without taxing it, and to be consistent was the first law of politics. So he stuck to it that they'd left it out uninten-tional and would be certain to do their best to fix it before they got caught and laughed at.

But I didn't feel no more interest in such things, as long as we couldn't git our sand through, and it made me low-spirited, and Jim the same. Tom he tried to cheer us up by say-ing he would think up another speculation for us that would be just as good as this one and

better, but it didn't do no good, we didn't believe there was any as big as this. It was mighty
hard; such a little while ago we was so rich, and
could 'a' bought a country and started a king-
dom and been celebrated and happy, and now
we was so poor and ornery again, and had our
sand left on our hands. The sand was looking
so lovely before, just like gold and di'monds,
and the feel of it was so soft and so silky and
nice, but now I couldn't bear the sight of it, it
made me sick to look at it, and I knowed I
wouldn't ever feel comfortable again till we got
shut of it, and I didn't have it there no more to
remind us of what we had been and what we had
got degraded down to. The others was feeling
the same way about it that I was. I knowed it,
because they cheered up so, the minute I says
le's throw this truck overboard.

Well, it was going to be work, you know, and
pretty solid work, too; so Tom he divided it up
according to fairness and strength. He said me
and him would clear out a fifth apiece of the
sand, and Jim three-fifths. Jim he didn't quite
like that arrangement. He says:

" 'Course I's de stronges', en I's willin' to do a
share accordin', but by jings you's kinder pilin'

it onto ole Jim, Mars Tom, hain't you?"

"Well, I didn't think so, Jim, but you try your hand at fixing it, and let's see."

So Jim reckoned it wouldn't be no more than fair if me and Tom done a *tenth* apiece. Tom he turned his back to git room and be private, and then he smole a smile that spread around and covered the whole Sahara to the westward, back to the Atlantic edge of it where we come from. Then he turned around again and said it was a good enough arrangement, and we was satisfied if Jim was. Jim said he was.

So then Tom measured off our two-tenths in the bow and left the rest for Jim, and it surprised Jim a good deal to see how much difference there was and what a raging lot of sand his share come to, and said he was powerful glad now that he had spoke up in time and got the first arrangement altered, for he said that even the way it was now, there was more sand than enjoyment in his end of the contract, he believed.

Then we laid into it. It was mighty hot work, and tough; so hot we had to move up into cooler weather or we couldn't 'a' stood it. Me and Tom took turn about, and one worked while t'other rested, but there warn't nobody to spell poor old Jim, and he made all that part of Africa damp, he sweated so. We couldn't work good, we was so full of laugh, and Jim he kept fretting and wanting to know what tickled us so, and we had to keep making up things to account for it, and they was pretty poor inventions, but they done well enough, Jim didn't see through them. At last when we got done we was 'most dead, but not with work but with laughing. By and by Jim was 'most dead, too, but it was with work; then we took turns and spelled him, and he was as thankful as he could be, and would set on the gunnel and swab the sweat, and heave and pant, and say how good we was to a poor old darky, and he wouldn't ever forgit us. He was always the gratefulest darky I ever see, for any little thing you done for him. He was only black outside; inside he was as white as you be.

12: *Jim Standing Siege*

THE next few meals was pretty sandy, but that don't make no difference when you are hungry; and when you ain't it ain't no satisfaction to eat, anyway, and so a little grit in the meat ain't no particular drawback, as far as I can see.

Then we struck the east end of the desert at last, sailing on a northeast course. Away off on the edge of the sand, in a soft pinky light, we see three little sharp roofs like tents, and Tom says:

"It's the pyramids of Egypt."

It made my heart fairly jump. You see, I had seen a many and a many a picture of them, and heard tell about them a hundred times, and yet

to come on them all of a sudden, that way, and
find they was *real*, 'stead of imaginations, 'most
knocked the breath out of me with surprise.
It's a curious thing, that the more you hear
about a grand and big and bully thing or person, the more it kind of dreamies out, as you
may say, and gets to be a big dim wavery figger
made out of moonshine and nothing solid to it.
It's just so with George Washington, and the
same with them pyramids.

And moreover, besides the thing they always
said about them seemed to me to be stretchers.
There was a feller come to the Sunday-school
once, and had a picture of them, and made a
speech, and said the biggest pyramid covered
thirteen acres, and was 'most five hundred foot
high, just a steep mountain, all built out of
hunks of stone as big as a bureau, and laid up in
perfectly regular layers, like stair-steps. Thirteen acres, you see, for just one building; it's a
farm. If it hadn't been in Sunday-school, I
would 'a' judged it was a lie; and outside I was
certain of it. And he said there was a hole in the
pyramid, and you could go in there with can-
dles, and go ever so far up a long slanting tunnel, and come to a large room in the stomach of

that stone mountain, and there you would find a big stone chest with a king in it, four thousand years old. I said to myself, then, if that ain't a lie I will eat that king if they will fetch him, for even Methusalem warn't that old, and nobody claims it.

As we come a little nearer we see the yaller sand come to an end in a long straight edge like a blanket, and onto it was joined, edge to edge, a wide country of bright green, with a snaky stripe crooking through it, and Tom said it was the Nile. It made my heart jump again, for the Nile was another thing that wasn't real to me. Now I can tell you one thing which is dead certain: if you will fool along over three thousand miles of yaller sand, all glimmering with heat so that it makes your eyes water to look at it, and you've been a considerable part of a week doing it, the green country will look so like home and heaven to you that it will make your eyes water *again*.

It was just so with me, and the same with Jim.

And when Jim got so he could believe it *was* the land of Egypt he was looking at, he wouldn't enter it standing up, but got down on his knees and took off his hat, because he said it wasn't fitten' for a humble poor darky to come any other way where such men had been as Moses and Joseph and Pharaoh and the other prophets. He was a Presbyterian, and had a most deep respect for Moses, which was a Presbyterian, too, he said.   He was all stirred up, and says:

"Hit's de lan' of Egypt, de lan' of Egypt, en I's 'lowed to look at it wid my own eyes! En dah's de river dat was turn' to blood, en I's looking at de very same groun' whah de plagues was, and de lice, en de frogs, en de locus', en de hail, en whah dey marked de door-pos', en de angel o' de Lord come by in de darkness o' de night en slew de fust-born in all de lan' o' Egypt. Ole Jim ain't worthy to see dis day!"

And then he just broke down and cried, he was so thankful.   So between him and Tom there was talk enough, Jim being excited because the land was so full of history—Joseph and his brethren, Moses in the bulrushers, Jacob coming down into Egypt to buy corn, the silver cup in the sack, and all them interesting things; and Tom just as excited too, because the land was so full of history that was in *his* line,

about Noureddin, and Bedreddin, and such like
monstrous giants, that made Jim's wool rise,
and a raft of other *Arabian Nights* folks, which
the half of them never done the things they let
on they done, I don't believe.

Then we struck a disappointment, for one of
them early morning fogs started up, and it
warn't no use to sail over the top of it, because
we would go by Egypt, sure, so we judged it was
best to set her by compass straight for the place
where the pyramids was gitting blurred and
blotted out, and then drop low and skin along
pretty close to the ground and keep a sharp
lookout. Tom took the hellum, I stood by to let
go the anchor, and Jim he straddled the bow to
dig through the fog with his eyes and watch out
for danger ahead. We went along a steady gait,
but not very fast, and the fog got solider and
solider, so solid that Jim looked dim and ragged
and smoky through it. It was awful still, and we
talked low and was anxious. Now and then Jim
would say:

"Highst her a p'int, Mars Tom, highst her!"
and up she would skip, a foot or two, and we
would slide right over a flat-roofed mud cabin,
with people that had been asleep on it just be-

ginning to turn out and gap and stretch; and once when a feller was clear up on his hind legs so he could gap and stretch better, we took him a blip in the back and knocked him off. By and by, after about an hour, and everything dead still and we a-straining our ears for sounds and holding our breath, the fog thinned a little, very sudden, and Jim sung out in an awful scare:

"Oh, for de lan's sake, set her back, Mars Tom, here's de biggest giant outen de *'Rabian Nights* a-comin' for us!" and he went over backwards in the boat.

Tom slammed on the back-action, and as we slowed to a standstill a man's face as big as our house at home looked in over the gunnel, same as a house looks out of its windows, and I laid down and died. I must 'a' been clear dead and gone for as much as a minute or more; then I come to, and Tom had hitched a boat-hook onto the lower lip of the giant and was holding the balloon steady with it whilst he canted his head back and got a good long look up at that awful face.

Jim was on his knees with his hands clasped, gazing up at the thing in a begging way, and working his lips, but not getting anything out.

I took only just a glimpse, and was fading out again, but Tom says:

"He ain't alive, you fools; it's the Sphinx!"

I never see Tom look so little and like a fly; but that was because the giant's head was so big and awful. Awful, yes, so it was, but not dreadful any more, because you could see it was a noble face, and kind of sad, and not thinking about you, but about other things and larger. It was stone, reddish stone, and its nose and ears battered, and that give it an abused look, and you felt sorrier for it for that.

We stood off a piece, and sailed around it and over it, and it was just grand. It was a man's head, or maybe a woman's, on a tiger's body a hundred and twenty-five foot long, and there was a dear little temple between its front paws. All but the head used to be under the sand, for hundreds of years, maybe thousands, but they had just lately dug the sand away and found that little temple. It took a power of sand to bury that cretur; 'most as much as it would to bury a steamboat, I reckon.

We landed Jim on top of the head, with an American flag to protect him, it being a foreign land; then we sailed off to this and that and t'other distance, to git what Tom called effects and perspectives and proportions, and Jim he done the best he could, striking all the different kinds of attitudes and positions he could study up, but standing on his head and working his legs the way a frog does was the best.   The further we got away, the littler Jim got, and the grander the Sphinx got, till at last it was only a clothes-pin on a dome, you might say.   That's the way perspective brings out the correct proportions, Tom said; he said Julus Cesar's slaves didn't know how big he was, they was too close to him.

Then we sailed off further and further, till we couldn't see Jim at all any more, and then that great figger was at its noblest, a-gazing out over the Nile Valley so still and solemn and lonesome, and all the little shabby huts and things that was scattered about it clean disappeared and gone, and nothing around it now but a soft wide spread of yaller velvet, which was the sand.

That was the right place to stop, and we done it.   We set there a-looking and a-thinking for a half an hour, nobody a-saying anything, for it made us feel quiet and kind of solemn to remember it had been looking over that valley just that same way, and thinking its awful thoughts all to itself for thousands of years, and nobody can't find out what they are to this day.

At last I took up the glass and see some little black things a-capering around on that velvet carpet, and some more a-climbing up the cretur's back, and then I see two or three wee puffs of white smoke, and told Tom to look. He done it, and says:

"They're bugs.   No—hold on; they—why, I believe they're men.   Yes, it's men—men and horses both.   They're hauling a long ladder up onto the Sphinx's back—now ain't that odd? And now they're trying to lean it up a—there's some more puffs of smoke—it's guns!   Huck, they're after Jim."

We clapped on the power, and went for them a-biling.   We was there in no time, and come a-whizzing down amongst them, and they broke and scattered every which way, and some that was climbing the ladder after Jim let go all holts and fell.   We soared up and found him laying on top of the head panting and most tuckered out, partly from howling for help and partly from scare.   He had been standing a siege a long time—a week, *he* said, but it warn't so, it only just seemed so to him because they was crowding him so. They had shot at him, and rained the bullets all around him, but he warn't hit, and when they found he wouldn't stand up and the bullets couldn't git at him when he was laying down, they went for the ladder, and then he knowed it was all up with him if we didn't come pretty quick. Tom was very indignant, and asked him why he didn't show the flag and command them to *git,* in the name of the United States. Jim said he done it, but they never paid no attention. Tom said he would have this thing looked into at Washington, and says:

"You'll see that they'll have to apologize for insulting the flag, and pay an indemnity, too, on top of it, even if they git off *that* easy."

Jim says:

"What's an indemnity, Mars Tom?"

"It's cash, that's what it is."

"Who gits it, Mars Tom?"

"Why, *we* do."

"En who gits de apology?"

"The United States. Or, we can take whichever we please. We can take the apology, if we want to, and let the gov'ment take the money."

"How much money will it be, Mars Tom?"

"Well, in an aggravated case like this one, it will be at least three dollars apiece, and I don't know but more."

"Well, den, we'll take de money, Mars Tom, blame de 'pology. Hain't dat yo' notion, too? En hain't it yourn, Huck?"

We talked it over a little and allowed that that was as good a way as any, so we agreed to take the money. It was a new business to me, and I asked Tom if countries always apologized when they had done wrong, and he says:

"Yes; the little ones does."

We was sailing around examining the pyramids, you know, and now we soared up and roosted on the flat top of the biggest one, and found it was just like what the man said in the Sunday-school. It was like four pairs of stairs that start broad at the bottom and slants up and comes together in a point at the top, only these stair-steps couldn't be clumb the way you climb other stairs; no, for each step was as high as your chin, and you have to be boosted up from behind. The two other pyramids warn't far away, and the people moving about on the sand between looked like bugs crawling, we was so high above them.

Tom he couldn't hold himself he was so worked up with gladness and astonishment to be in such a celebrated place, and he just dripped history from every pore, seemed to me. He said he couldn't scarcely believe he was standing on the very identical spot the prince flew from on the Bronze Horse. It was in the *Arabian Night* times, he said. Somebody give the prince a bronze horse with a peg in its shoulder, and he could git on him and fly through the air like a bird, and go all over the world, and steer it by turning the peg, and fly high or low and land wherever he wanted to.

When he got done telling it there was one of them uncomfortable silences that comes, you know, when a person has been telling a whopper and you feel sorry for him and wish you could think of some way to change the subject and let him down easy, but git stuck and don't see no way, and before you can pull your mind together and *do* something, that silence has got in and spared itself and done the business. I was embarrassed, Jim he was embarrassed, and neither of us couldn't say a word.

Well, Tom he glowered at me a minute, and says:

"Come, out with it. What do you think?"

I says:

"Tom Sawyer, *you* don't believe that, yourself."

"What's the reason I don't? What's to hender me?"

"There's one thing to hender you: it couldn't happen, that's all."

"What's the reason it couldn't happen?"

"You tell me the reason it *could* happen."

"This balloon is a good enough reason it could happen, I should reckon."

"*Why* is it?"

"*Why* is it? I never saw such an idiot. Ain't this balloon and the bronze horse the same thing under different names?"

"No, they're not. One is a balloon and the other's a horse. It's very different. Next you'll be saying a house and a cow is the same thing."

"By Jackson, Huck's got him ag'in! Dey ain't no wigglin' outer dat!"

"Shut your head, Jim; you don't know what you're talking about. And Huck don't. Look here, Huck, I'll make it plain to you, so you can understand. You see, it ain't the mere *form* that's got anything to do with their being similar or unsimilar, it's the *principle* involved; and the principle is the same in both. Don't you see, now?"

I turned it over in my mind, and says:

"Tom, it ain't no use. Principles is all very well, but they don't git around that one big fact, that the thing that a balloon can do ain't no sort of proof of what a horse can do."

"Shucks, Huck, you don't get the idea at all. Now look here a minute—it's perfectly plain. Don't we fly through the air?"

"Yes."

"Very well. Don't we fly high or fly low, just as we please?"

"Yes."

"Don't we steer whichever way we want to?"

"Yes."

"And don't we land when and where we please?"

"Yes."

"How do we move the balloon and steer it?"

"By touching the buttons."

"*Now* I reckon the thing is clear to you at last.

In the other case the moving and steering was done by turning a peg. We touch a button, the prince turned a peg. There ain't an atom of difference, you see. I knowed I could git it through your head if I stuck to it long enough."

He felt so happy he begun to whistle. But me and Jim was silent, so he broke off surprised, and says:

"Looky here, Huck Finn, don't you see it yet?"

I says:

"Tom Sawyer, I want to ask you some questions."

"Go ahead," he says, and I see Jim chirk up to listen.

"As I understand it, the whole thing is in the buttons and the peg—the rest ain't of no consequence. A button is one shape, a peg is another shape, but that ain't any matter?"

"No, that ain't any matter, as long as they've both got the same power."

"All right, then. What is the power that's in a candle and in a match?"

"It's the fire."

"It's the same in both, then?"

"Yes, just the same in both."

"All right. Suppose I set fire to a carpenter shop with a match, what will happen to that carpenter shop?"

"She'll burn up."

"And suppose I set fire to this pyramid with a candle—will she burn up?"

"Of course she won't."

"All right. Now the fire's the same, both times. *Why* does the shop burn, and the pyramid don't?"

"Because the pyramid *can't* burn."

"Ah! and *a horse can't fly!*"

"My lan', ef Huck ain't got him ag'in! Huck's landed him high en dry dis time, *I* tell you! Hit's de smartes' trap I ever see a body walk inter—en ef I—"

But Jim was so full of laugh he got to strangling and couldn't go on, and Tom was that mad to see how neat I had floored him, and turned his own argument ag'in him and knocked him all to rags and flinders with it, that all he could manage to say was that whenever he heard me and Jim try to argue it made him ashamed of the human race. I never said nothing; I was feeling pretty well satisfied. When I have got the best of a person that way, it ain't my way to go around crowing about it the way some people does, for I consider that if I was in his place I wouldn't wish him to crow over me. It's better to be generous, that's what I think.

13: *Going for Tom's Pipe*

By and by we left Jim to float around up there
in the neighborhood of the pyramids, and we
clumb down to the hole where you go into the
tunnel, and went in with some Arabs and can-
dles, and away in there in the middle of the
pyramid we found a room and a big stone box in
it where they used to keep that king, just as the
man in the Sunday-school said; but he was gone,
now; somebody had got him. But I didn't take
no interest in the place, because there could be
ghosts there, of course; not fresh ones, but I
don't like no kind.

So then we come out and got some little donkeys and rode a piece, and then went in a boat
another piece, and then more donkeys, and got
to Cairo; and all the way the road was as smooth
and beautiful a road as ever I see, and had tall
date-pa'ms on both sides, and naked children
everywhere, and the men was as red as copper,
and fine and strong and handsome. And the
city was a curiosity. Such narrow streets—why,
they were just lanes, and crowded with people
with turbans, and women with veils, and everybody rigged out in blazing bright clothes and all
sorts of colors, and you wondered how the camels and the people got by each other in such
narrow little cracks, but they done it—a perfect
jam, you see, and everybody noisy. The stores
warn't big enough to turn around in, but you
didn't have to go in; the storekeeper sat tailor
fashion on his counter, smoking his snaky long
pipe, and had his things where he could reach
them to sell, and he was just as good as in the
street, for the camel-loads brushed him as they
went by.

Now and then a grand person flew by in a
carriage with fancy dressed men running and
yelling in front of it and whacking anybody

*Everybody was rigged out in blazing bright
clothes and all sorts of colors*

with a long rod that didn't get out of the way.
And by and by along comes the Sultan riding
horseback at the head of a procession, and fairly
took your breath away, his clothes was so splendid; and everybody fell flat and laid on his
stomach while he went by.   I forgot, but a feller
helped me to remember.   He was one that had a
rod and run in front.

There was churches, but they don't know
enough to keep Sunday; they keep Friday and
break the Sabbath.   You have to take off your
shoes when you go in.   There was crowds of
men and boys in the church, setting in groups
on the stone floor and making no end of noise—
getting their lessons by heart, Tom said, out of
the Koran, which they think is a Bible, and
people that knows better knows enough to not
let on.   I never see such a big church in my life
before, and most awful high, it was; it made you
dizzy to look up; our village church at home
ain't a circumstance to it; if you was to put it in
there, people would think it was a dry-goods
box.

What I wanted to see was a dervish, because I
was interested in dervishes on account of the
one that played the trick on the camel-driver.

So we found a lot in a kind of a church, and they
called themselves Whirling Dervishes; and they
did whirl, too.   I never see anything like it.
They had tall sugar-loaf hats on, and linen petticoats; and they spun and spun and spun, round
and round like tops, and the petticoats stood out
on a slant, and it was the prettiest thing I ever
see, and made me drunk to look at it.   They was
all Moslems, Tom said, and when I asked him
what a Moslem was, he said it was a person that
wasn't a Presbyterian.   So there is plenty of
them in Missouri, though I didn't know it before.

We didn't see half there was to see in Cairo,
because Tom was in such a sweat to hunt out
places that was celebrated in history.   We had a
most tiresome time to find the granary where
Joseph stored up the grain before the famine,
and when we found it it warn't worth much to
look at, being such an old tumbledown wreck;
but Tom was satisfied, and made more fuss over
it than I would make if I stuck a nail in my foot.
How he ever found that place was too many for
me.   We passed as much as forty just like it
before we come to it, and any of them would 'a'
done for me, but none but just the right one

would suit him; I never see anybody so particular as Tom Sawyer. The minute he struck the
right one he reconnized it as easy as I would
reconnize my other shirt if I had one, but how
he done it he couldn't any more tell than he
could fly; he said so himself.

Then we hunted a long time for the house
where the boy lived that learned the cadi how to
try the case of the old olives and the new ones,
and said it was out of the *Arabian Nights,* and
he would tell me and Jim about it when he got
time. Well, we hunted and hunted till I was
ready to drop, and I wanted Tom to give it up
and come next day and git somebody that
knowed the town and could talk Missourian
and could go straight to the place; but no, he
wanted to find it himself, and nothing else
would answer. So on we went. Then at last
the remarkablest thing happened I ever see.
The house was gone—gone hundreds of years
ago—every last rag of it gone but just one mud
brick. Now a person wouldn't ever believe that
a backwoods Missouri boy that hadn't ever been
in that town before could go and hunt
that place over and find that brick, but Tom
Sawyer done it. I know he done it, because I

see him do it.   I was right by his very side at the
time, and see him see the brick and see him
reconnize it.   Well, I says to myself, how *does* he
do it?   Is it knowledge, or is it instink?

Now there's the facts, just as they happened:
let everybody explain it their own way.   I've
ciphered over it a good deal, and it's my opinion
that some of it is knowledge but the main bulk
of it is instink.   The reason is this: Tom put
the brick in his pocket to give to a museum with
his name on it and the facts when he went home,
and I slipped it out and put another brick considerable like it in its place, and he didn't know
the difference—but there was a difference, you
see.   I think that settles it—it's mostly instink,
not knowledge.   Instink tells him where the
exact *place* is for the brick to be in, and so he
reconnizes it by the place it's in, not by the look
of the brick.   If it was knowledge, not instink,
he would know the brick again by the look of it
the next time he seen it—which he didn't.   So it
shows that for all the brag you hear about
knowledge being such a wonderful thing, instink is worth forty of it for real unerringness.
Jim says the same.

When we got back Jim dropped down and

took us in, and there was a young man there
with a red skull-cap and tassel on and a beautiful silk jacket and baggy trousers with a shawl
around his waist and pistols in it that could talk
English and wanted to hire to us as guide and
take us to Mecca and Medina and Central
Africa and everywheres for a half a dollar a day
and his keep, and we hired him and left, and
piled on the power, and by the time we was
through dinner we was over the place where the
Israelites crossed the Red Sea when Pharaoh
tried to overtake them and was caught by the
waters.   We stopped, then, and had a good look
at the place, and it done Jim good to see it.   He
said he could see it all, now, just the way it
happened; he could see the Israelites walking
along between the walls of water, and the Egyp-
tians coming, from away off yonder, hurrying
all they could, and see them start in as the Israelites went out, and then when they was all in, see
the walls tumble together and drown the last
man of them.   Then we piled on the power
again and rushed away and huvvered over
Mount Sinai, and saw the place where Moses
broke the tables of stone, and where the children of Israel camped in the plain and

worshiped the golden calf, and it was all just as interesting as could be, and the guide knowed every place as well as I knowed the village at home.

But we had an accident, now, and it fetched all the plans to a standstill. Tom's old ornery corn-cob pipe had got so old and swelled and warped that she couldn't hold together any longer, notwithstanding the strings and bandages, but caved in and went to pieces. Tom he didn't know *what* to do. The professor's pipe wouldn't answer; it warn't anything but a mershum, and a person that's got used to a cob pipe knows it lays a long ways over all the other pipes in this world, and you can't git him to smoke any other. He wouldn't take mine, I couldn't persuade him. So there he was.

He thought it over, and said we must scour around and see if we could roust out one in Egypt or Arabia or around in some of these countries, but the guide said no, it warn't no use, they didn't have them. So Tom was pretty glum for a little while, then he chirked up and said he'd got the idea and knowed what to do. He says:

"I've got another corn-cob pipe, and it's a

prime one, too, and nearly new. It's laying on
the rafter that's right over the kitchen stove at
home in the village. Jim, you and the guide
will go and get it, and me and Huck will camp
here on Mount Sinai till you come back."

"But, Mars Tom, we couldn't ever find de
village. I could find de pipe, 'case I knows de
kitchen, but, my lan', we can't ever find de village, nur Sent Louis, nur none o' dem places.
We don't know de way, Mars Tom."

That was a fact, and it stumped Tom for a
minute. Then he said:

"Looky here, it can be done, sure; and I'll tell
you how. You set your compass and sail west as
straight as a dart, till you find the United States.
It ain't any trouble, because it's the first land
you'll strike the other side of the Atlantic. If it's
daytime when you strike it, bulge right on,
straight west from the upper part of the Florida
coast, and in an hour and three-quarters you'll
hit the mouth of the Mississippi—at the speed
that I'm going to send you. You'll be so high up
in the air that the earth will be curved considerable—sorter like a washbowl turned upside
down—and you'll see a raft of rivers crawling
around every which way, long before you get

there, and you can pick out the Mississippi without any trouble. Then you can follow the river north nearly, an hour and three-quarters, till you see the Ohio come in; then you want to look sharp, because you're getting near. Away up to your left you'll see another thread coming in— that's the Missouri and is a little above St. Louis. You'll come down low then, so as you can examine the villages as you spin along. You'll pass about twenty-five in the next fifteen minutes, and you'll recognize ours when you see it—and if you don't you can yell down and ask."

"Ef it's dat easy, Mars Tom, I reckon we kin do it—yassir, I knows we kin."

The guide was sure of it, too, and thought that he could learn to stand his watch in a little while.

"Jim can learn you the whole thing in a half an hour," Tom said. "This balloon's as easy to manage as a canoe."

Tom got out the chart and marked out the course and measured it, and says:

"To go back west is the shortest way, you see. It's only about seven thousand miles. If you

went east, and so on around, it's over twice as
far." Then he says to the guide, "I want you
both to watch the telltale all through the
watches, and whenever it don't mark three hundred miles an hour, you go higher or drop lower
till you find a storm-current that's going your
way. There's a hundred miles an hour in this
old thing without any wind to help. There's
two-hundred mile gales to be found, any time
you want to hunt for them."

"We'll hunt for them, sir."

"See that you do. Sometimes you may have
to go up a couple of miles, and it'll be p'ison
cold, but most of the time you'll find your storm
a good deal lower. If you can only strike a
cyclone—that's the ticket for you! You'll see
by the professor's books that they travel west in
these latitudes; and they travel low, too."

Then he ciphered on the time, and says:

"Seven thousand miles, three hundred miles
an hour—you can make the trip in a day—
twenty-four hours. This is Thursday; you'll be
back here Saturday afternoon. Come, now,
hustle out some blankets and food and books
and things for me and Huck, and you can start

right along.   There ain't no occasion to fool
around—I want a smoke, and the quicker you
fetch that pipe the better."

All hands jumped for the things, and in eight
minutes our things was out and the balloon
was ready for America.   So we shook hands
good-by, and Tom gave his last orders:

"It's ten minutes to 2 P.M. now, Mount Sinai
time.   In twenty-four hours you'll be home, and
it'll be six tomorrow morning, village time.
When you strike the village, land a little back of
the top of the hill, in the woods, out of sight;
then you rush down, Jim, and shove these letters in the post-office, and if you see anybody
stirring, pull your slouch down over your face so
they won't know you.   Then you go and slip in
the back way to the kitchen and git the pipe,
and lay this piece of paper on the kitchen table,
and put something on it to hold it, and then
slide out and git away, and don't let Aunt Polly
catch a sight of you, nor nobody else.   Then
you jump for the balloon and shove for Mount
Sinai three hundred miles an hour.   You won't
have lost more than an hour.   You'll start back
at 7 or 8 A.M., village time, and be here in twenty-

four hours, arriving at 2 or 3 P.M., Mount Sinai time."

Tom he read the piece of paper to us. He had wrote on it:

"THURSDAY AFTERNOON. *Tom Sawyer the Erronort sends his love to Aunt Polly from Mount Sinai where the Ark was,*[1] *and so does Huck Finn, and she will get it tomorrow morning half-past six.*

"TOM SAWYER THE ERRONORT."

"That'll make her eyes bulge out and the tears come," he says. Then he says:

"Stand by! One—two—three—away you go!"

And away she *did* go! Why, she seemed to whiz out of sight in a second.

Then we found a most comfortable cave that looked out over the whole big plain, and there we camped to wait for the pipe.

The balloon come back all right, and brung the pipe; but Aunt Polly had catched Jim when he was getting it, and anybody can guess what happened: she sent for Tom. So Jim he says:

---

[1] This misplacing of the Ark is probably Huck's error, not Tom's.—M. T.

"Mars Tom, she's out on de porch wid her eye sot on de sky a-layin' for you, en she say she ain't gwyne to budge from dah tell she gits hold of you.   Dey's gwyne to be trouble, Mars Tom, 'deed dey is."

So then we shoved for home, and not feeling very gay, neither.